[redacted]

Grosse Pointe Girl

Tales from a Suburban Adolescence

Sarah Grace McCandless

Illustrated by Christine Norrie

Simon & Schuster Paperbacks

New York   London   Toronto   Sydney

SIMON & SCHUSTER PAPERBACKS
Rockefeller Center
1230 Avenue of the Americas
New York, NY 10020

First Simon & Schuster trade paperback edition 2004

SIMON & SCHUSTER and colophon are registered trademarks
of Simon & Schuster, Inc.

Book design by Ellen R. Sasahara

Manufactured in the United States of America

10 9 8 7 6 5 4 3 2

Library of Congress Cataloging-in-Publication Data

McCandless, Sarah Grace.
    Grosse Pointe girl : tales from a suburban adolescence / Sarah
    Grace McCandless ; illustrated by Christine Norrie.—1st Simon &
    Schuster trade pbk. ed.
        p. cm.
    1. Grosse Pointe (Mich.)—Fiction. 2. Suburban life—Fiction.
    3. Teenage girls—Fiction. I. Title.
    PS3613.C34525G76 2004
    813'.6—dc22
    2004041637

ISBN 0-7432-5612-3 (pbk.)

For information regarding special discounts for bulk purchases,
please contact Simon & Schuster Special Sales at 1-800-456-6798
or business@simonandschuster.com

For Drew Woodruff

Acknowledgments

First, my never-ending gratitude goes out to Jenny Bent, the best agent a girl could ask for, as well as the foremost expert on the best fountain sodas in the New York City area.

Denise Roy, you are not just the most fabulous editor in all the land but my psychic friend, favorite cousin, therapist, sorority sister, and personal stylist all rolled into one. Thank you for talking me off the ledge more than once. I have been blessed under your guidance.

Also many thanks to Christina "Xtina" Richardson, Victoria Meyer, David Rosenthal, and everyone at Simon & Schuster.

Christine Norrie, you are a brilliant artist and I am forever in awe of your talent.

To my unofficial editors/guidance counselors/mentors, Pam Houston, Joe Weisberg, and Shawn McBride: You are royalty. And many thanks to the others who continue to inspire me, especially Lorrie Moore, Thisbe Nissen, Melissa Bank, Peter Hedges, Carolyn Forché, Jeffrey Eugenides, Michael Chabon, Cameron Crowe, Ryan Adams, and Adam Duritz.

The following are just a few of those who've offered invaluable support and advice:

Ritah Parrish, Kevin Sampsell, and Future Tense Books; Michael Murphy; the Multnomah County Library & Sterling Room for Writers; Chris Erb; Chris Pfeifer at Tonic Industries;

the "Coming Out in Creede" 2002 workshop participants—you know who you are; my girls Carey Black, Misty Osko ("It's all happening"), Kimberly McFarland; my other "girls" Tim Williams and Chris Cerasi.

I am eternally grateful to Lee Dawson for pushing me to do this in the first place.

Many, many thanks to everyone at Dark Horse Comics, especially Scott "the Escapist" Allie, Cary Grazzini, Mring, Cara Niece, and Jeff Macey for the unofficial GPG soundtrack. Mucho gratitude to my other pals from the comics world, including but not limited to Jamie Rich and the Oni Press gang, Chris Staros from Top Shelf, Bozzi, Phil Amara, Casey Seijas, Eric Powell, Adam Gallardo, Chris Oarr, and Rich Johnson. And a special shout out to Ian Sattler—your drive is impressive and addictive, setting the standard of what is possible; it makes me want to rise to the occasion.

Heartfelt thanks to all Pointers past and present, especially Jimmy Fillmore, Heather King, Karin Mueller, Jeff Osborne, Alex Papapanos, Carla Slomski, and Stephe Walsh.

And last but not least, big ups to the McCandless family and the Harrison family. One love y'all.

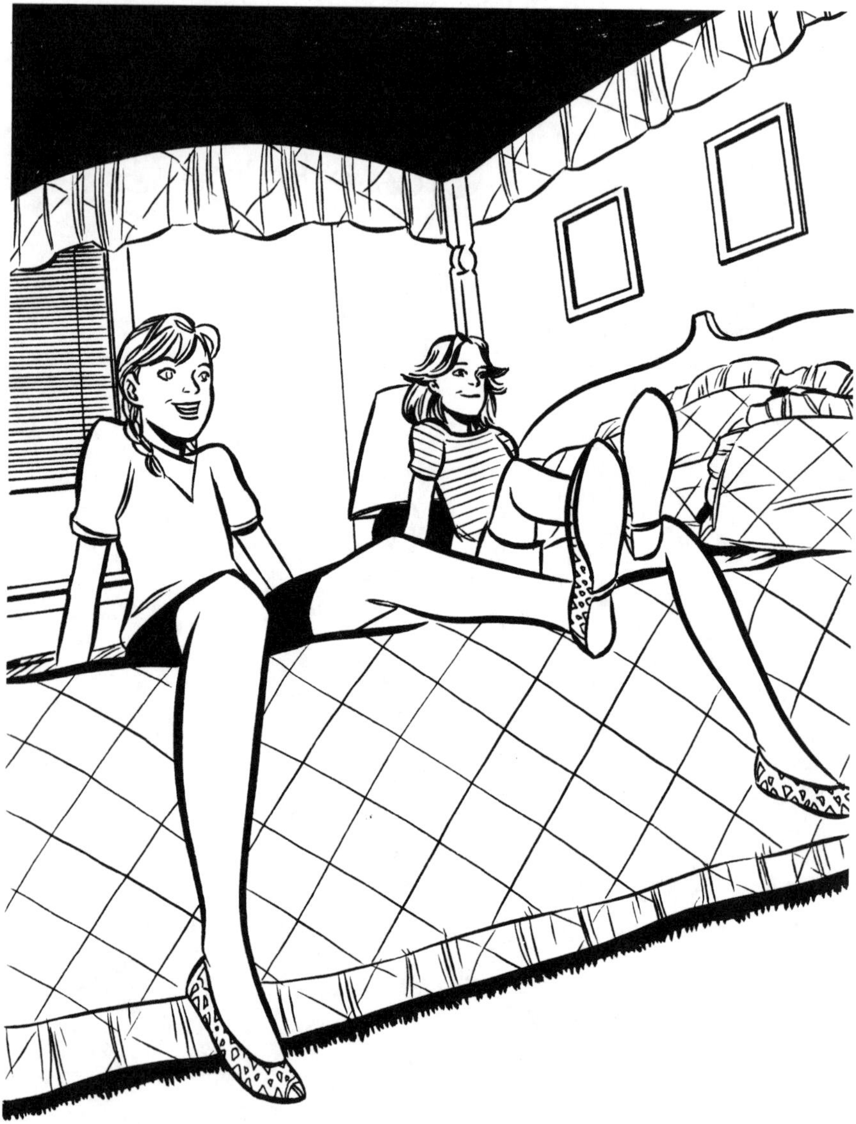

Welcome to Grosse Pointe

"Hi," she says. "Sorry to block your sun."

I sit up and try to smooth out my T-shirt and hide my sweat stains. "Hi. I was just . . . resting for a minute." She's wearing pink plastic shoes, the exact ones I wanted from Lord & Taylor. Mom made me get the blue pair because they were on sale.

"I live next door," she tells me, like I don't know, carefully folding her legs under her body like a cloth napkin until she's beside me on the ground. Her toenails are polished in hot pink with flecks of glitter. On her left big toe, she wears a silver ring.

"I saw you earlier, in the window?" She says it like a question. "Your room is right across from mine." She starts to pick at the blades of grass, collecting the fragments in her palm. She's set her buttercup hair in a French braid, the weaves tight and precise.

"I could teach you how," she says, reading my mind.

"Emma, who are you talking to?" Mom calls over, taking her eyes off the movers for the first time since we arrived.

"Katrina," the buttercup girl whispers in my ear. She smells like peach Jolly Ranchers.

"Katrina," I yell back, trying to will my mother invisible or at least mute. "She lives next door."

"Okay, well you can visit for a little while but don't forget about your room," she says, flashing a toothpaste-commercial smile. Mom wants me to make a new friend so bad it's as obvious as when Shelly Green from my old school used to bribe us with Twinkies to eat at her lunch table.

"My mom sent me here to invite your family over for cocktails," Katrina tells me, apparently ignoring my own mother's lack of cool.

"Cocktails?" I repeat like it's a foreign word I don't understand. "Cocktails?" Now I'm a parrot.

"You know, drinks and cheese and crackers and all that, a sort of welcome-to-the-neighborhood-type thing. It's standard. Do you think you could come over at six?"

"I'll ask," I tell her, and then because it's the only thing I can think of, "There's a rerun of *Poltergeist* on at eight." There's a man inside installing our cable television. We've never had pay stations before.

"Yeah, we have Showtime too. I've seen *Poltergeist* three times. You think everything is going to turn out okay, but don't believe what you see," she tells me, lifting herself off the ground in one try.

She's halfway across the lawn when she stops and turns to ask, "Hey, what grade are you going into?"

"Sixth," I say.

"Cool. Me too," she says, and then she glides away like a sailboat in a light breeze.

The sky looks different from where Katrina has left me sitting in our front yard, closer and bluer and somehow as if I could reach up and make it my own. I check the time on the old Girl Scout watch I still wear. Technically, I've got a few minutes left on my break. But it's only six hours until cocktails, so I leap off the ground and race to tell Mom about the invitation. She might need a new friend in this town too, and if I'm lucky, I'll be able to find my blue plastic shoes in time.

★ ★ ★ ★ ★

Earlier this morning, when I took my spot next to my brother, Jack, in the backseat of our packed minivan, I immediately defined the boundaries. "This is MY side," I declared, my finger drawing a useless line between us. His hands, sticky from an orange Popsicle, hovered as close to my face as they could without actually making contact.

"Mom! He's touching me again!"

"No, I'm not. Technically, I'm not touching her," he said. Then came a squeaking sound and then the car stunk like bad eggs.

Jack's only two years older than I am. We used to play Clue together or Sorry, or sometimes even "Goonies," where we'd reenact hunting for One-Eyed Willie's treasure while keeping one step ahead of the bad guys. But now that he's going into his last year of middle school, it's just torture with his smells or holding me down to rub his dirty feet on me or punching me in the arm when I won't give him the remote control.

"If you want to go to the pool after we unpack, you'll knock it off!" Mom barked.

We'd been told that the new town had its own lakefront park with tennis courts, picnic tables, and even a high dive. Grosse Pointe was where my father grew up, just outside Detroit. After Mom yelled at us, Dad turned in his seat to tell me once again, "When it's time, Emma, you'll be going to the same high school I did."

"How long will it take to get there?" I asked him.

"About a half hour," he said.

"Keep your eyes on the road," Mom warned. Then she turned her right palm toward me as if it were a stop sign. In Michigan, we used this hand as a map. Mom pointed to the fleshy part below her thumb. "We live here," she said, then, shifting her finger slightly toward the edge, she explained, "and we're moving here."

I didn't see much of a difference. There were fine lines on her hand, highways to other parts of the state, and I wondered why we didn't take one of those roads that stretched out in another direction.

My legs, tanned and exposed midthigh in my jeans shorts, were already sticking to the upholstery even though the air-conditioning was turned to high. This car had real leather seats because of Dad's job. Like most Detroit-area parents, Dad worked for a major auto company, one of the "Big Three." He was always bringing home the newest cars for a test drive. This latest car had been a signing bonus when he'd switched from one company to another a few weeks ago. That was when Dad told us we were moving into an actual house. I hadn't seen it yet, but Mom said it had four bedrooms, two floors, and its own driveway.

"Do we have more money now?" I asked her as we merged onto the freeway.

"I guess," she answered, fixing her eye makeup in the visor mirror. "But there will always be others in Grosse Pointe who have more."

I wasn't sure what that meant.

Whenever we drive into Detroit, Mom clicks the locks to make sure we stay safe. Mostly I've seen only the edges of the city hugging the exit ramps, abandoned buildings padded with wads of yellowed newspapers that crouch until startled by the traffic. It didn't seem like a place anyone really lived, more like a dangerous obstacle course that warned, "Avoid downtown at night," or "Don't talk to anyone on the street," or "Never walk alone."

I didn't have to ask Dad when we crossed over Alter Road into Grosse Pointe. On the Detroit side, the lawns were brown and ragged. The front porches were missing planks of wood and the mail was piled up in the doorways. On the Grosse Pointe side, yards were as green as the plastic grass from an Easter basket. Houses announced their locations with brass numbers, secured tightly and in order. The flowers stood with confidence. I was convinced that invisible armed guards must have patrolled the streets of Grosse Pointe, burying land mines to keep out what did not belong.

Dad cracked his window and pushed in the cigarette lighter, then tapped out a smoke while waiting for it to pop. When it did, he kept one hand on the steering wheel and with the other cupped the bright, burning coil to the end of the stick hanging out of the corner of his mouth. My mother waved her hand in front of her nose like she always does, but Dad ignored her, blowing the smoke toward the other cars passing us by.

His silver-and-green pack sitting on the dashboard said

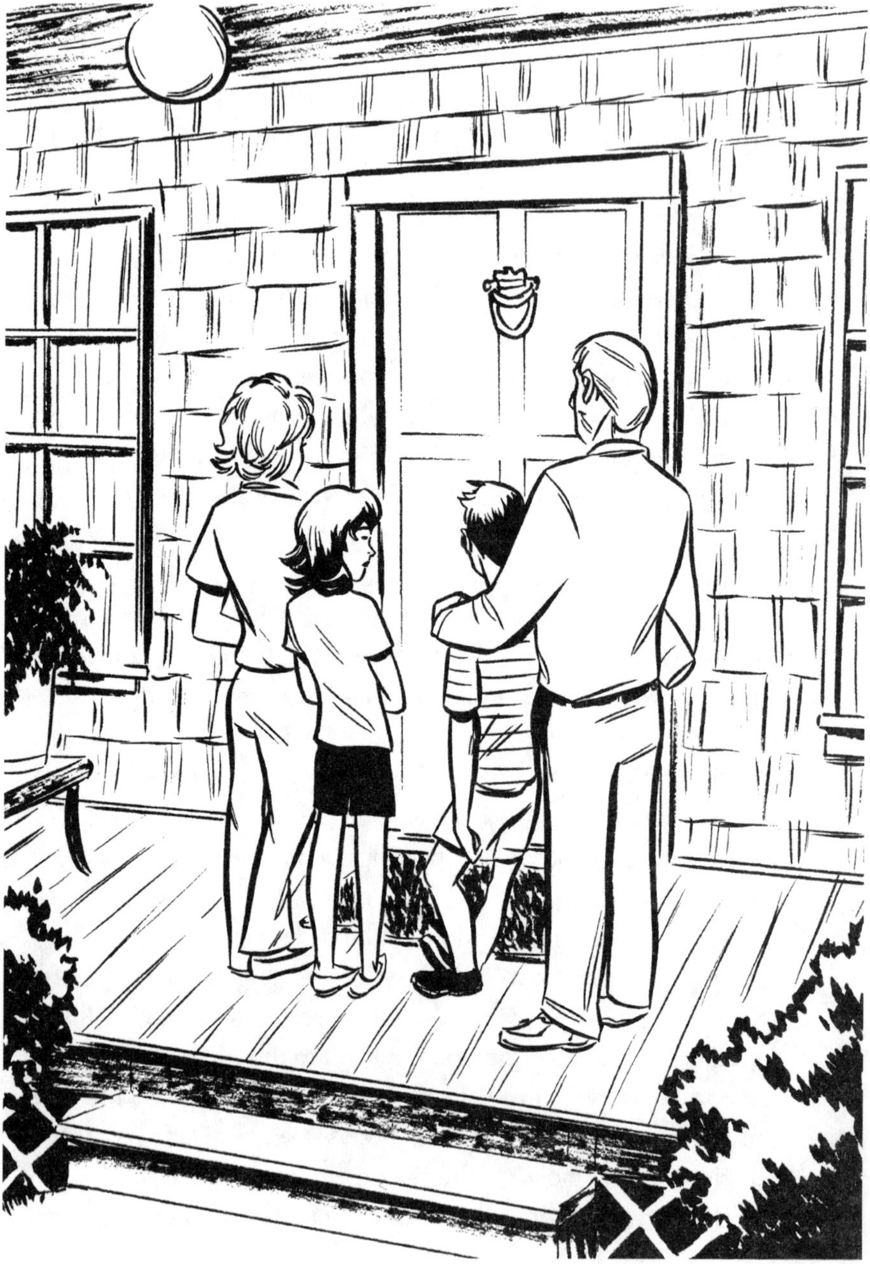

"Menthol." Dad once told me it meant they tasted minty, but I think they still smell exactly the same as usual.

* * * * *

At 6:01 P.M., my family stands, freshly showered, on Katrina's front porch. Our clean clothes are cobbled together from whatever we could find among the boxes and bags. My mother holds a blueberry torte she made Dad pick up from the bakery.

"Never arrive empty-handed," she says.

Dad clutches a bottle of vodka, the liquor as clear as water.

"Wine would have been more appropriate," Mom tells him for the third time.

"This is the nice stuff," he repeats, pushing the glowing doorbell.

A woman with short, feathered brown hair comes toward the screen door. "You must be our new neighbors," she says in soft syllables sprinkled with a foreign accent. "I'm Mrs. Liza Krause, Katrina's mother. Come on in."

Mrs. Liza Krause is wearing a strand of pearls. I watch my mother's hand float toward her own bare neck. As we pass through the door, they try to hug but it ends up being more of a lean, the torte creating a distance between them. My father shakes Mrs. Liza Krause's hand as if he's at a business meeting.

The living-room furniture is so pristine that the plastic covers must have been peeled off moments before we arrived. Trays of food are set out on top of the coffee table, green grapes plucked fresh from the stem, slices of thick white cheese, crackers shaped like butterflies.

Katrina's dad, who has introduced himself as Mark to my parents and Mr. Krause to me and Jack, says in the booming voice of a game-show host, "Make yourselves comfortable!" Dad hands him the bottle of vodka.

"Frank, I knew you were a martini man. How do you take it?"

"Dry, with an olive," Dad tells him, speaking in some sort of coded language they both understand.

Katrina enters the room. Her blond hair, released from its braid, falls in loose curls past her shoulders. She shakes my parents' hands and gives my brother a wave, then sits next to me on the piano bench.

"Do you play?" she asks, reaching toward the coffee table for food.

"I start lessons next week," I tell her. She has retrieved a handful of chilled grapes and places one in my palm. I roll it back and forth like a marble.

"I can give you the number of our teacher, Miss Malloy," Mrs. Liza Krause says to my mother, passing her a paper cocktail napkin printed with blue-and-green boat anchors. "Katrina's been studying with her for two years now. Katrina, why don't you play the concertino you've been working on?"

Katrina sighs but turns around to face the piano without argument. When she lifts the cover, I slide to the far end of the bench to give her more room. Her fingers—polished to match her toes—barely touch the keys as she taps out the flirty song. It only lasts a minute or two, but as far as I can tell, she doesn't make one mistake and when she finishes, everyone applauds politely.

Mrs. Liza Krause says to her husband, "Mark, fix Marianne a drink." I always pause when I hear someone call my mom by her first name, not sure for a moment who they are talking about. He hands Mom a cranberry-colored concoction called a seabreeze.

"Tart," my mother says on her first sip. "And good," she adds. Mrs. Liza Krause nods. "It's so refreshing in the summer." Mr. Krause and Dad are already refilling their martinis.

"So, Marianne," Mrs. Liza Krause says, her pearl necklace smiling at us like baby teeth. "What brings you to Grosse Pointe?"

My mother pauses to take a sip of her seabreeze. The sip turns into a gulp before she answers.

"Change."

* * * * *

The home we left behind wasn't exactly a house. It's what Mom called a "condo," but I think that was just a fancy word for apartment because everything was on one floor and there were people living above and below us. We weren't allowed to paint or put in new carpeting, so every room stayed the same color, like oatmeal left in a pot on the stove.

A maze of bike paths surrounded our apartment complex and without the threat of oncoming traffic Jack and I learned how to ride fast. The pond on the south side of the grounds was where Dad used to take us after he and Mom would fight. We'd bring bags of stale Wonder bread, dried-out torn pieces, to feed the ducks, then watch them circle and argue.

At twilight, we'd go back to the apartment. Dad would put on a Johnny Mathis record to try and make up with Mom. When it worked, Jack would use his instant camera to take pictures of them dancing.

Maybe as proof.

Sometimes, after the bus dropped Jack and me off from school, we'd find Mom in the apartment hiding behind the stiff,

---

tweed curtains that came with the place, holding the remains of whatever dessert we'd had the night before. Double-chocolate cake or fruit flan with kiwi or pumpkin pie (even if it wasn't Thanksgiving, it didn't matter). She'd clutch the entire porcelain plate, the one Grandma gave us, with edges like waves, and let her toes stick out on purpose so we'd pull the drapes aside. Then she would laugh, loud and full, handing over whatever was left.

By the time Dad got home from work, the dish would be washed clean and dried, ready for the next meal.

* * * * *

"I've learned how to adapt."

Mrs. Liza Krause tells us this as she stands at the record player, setting the needle down as a symphony fills the room.

"We're German, you know. First generation. Not exactly the standard here, but we picked the city for the school system and the parks. The safety."

"The school system IS terrific." Mr. Krause's voice has become louder with each drink. I've counted four refills so far. Dad has kept up, while Mom quietly switched to the iced tea Katrina and Jack and I have been sipping.

"And there's the Neighborhood Club," Mrs. Krause adds.

"What's that?" Mom asks.

"It's one of the community centers. You can take just about any class—tennis, SAT prep, painting. They have ice skating in the winter, and Little League in the summer. It's a good idea to get involved with the community."

"That sounds great," Mom says. She corrects herself. "That sounds lovely."

"Do you hunt, Frank?" Mr. Krause yells to my dad.

Before I can hear Dad's answer, Katrina whispers, "Don't go into our garage, ever. When my dad goes hunting, whatever he's killed is usually hanging from the rafters."

I'm wondering if she's lying just to scare me when she announces, "I'm going to show Emma my hamster. We'll be right back." I steal a glance at Jack, but he's building a triple-decker cheese-and-cracker sandwich.

Katrina's room is about the same as mine but she has her own bathroom—shower, toilet, sink, fluffy white towels hung evenly on the bar and monogrammed in pink and green. I look out her bedroom window, standing in the same spot I had seen her earlier in the day, before I knew her name or that she wore plastic jelly shoes or played concertinos.

Her hamster cage is in the corner. The fluffy caramel-colored rodent has stuffed itself in a yellow Habitrail tube. "What's its name?" I ask.

"Hammy," she says, as if it's the most obvious thing ever. "I had one before him but he got loose and died."

"What was the old one named?"

"Hammy," she says again. "It's just easier that way." She reaches into a plastic bag and drops a few food pellets into his dish. "Do you have a bike?"

"Yes," I tell her, looking at the Kirk Cameron and Poison posters taped to her closet door.

"We could ride bikes up to the drugstore tomorrow."

"Okay," I say. "I'll ask my mom. Is it in the Village?" I guess, trying to remember some of the areas of town Dad pointed out to me.

"No, in the Hill," she says. Damnit, I think. "It's not far."

Katrina's dresser top is flooded with jars of hair gel, tubes of colored lip gloss, and bottles of perfumes and nearly empty body sprays. Above it, there's a large horizontal mirror and from where we're standing next to each other, our heads are outside the frame. But in the reflection, I can clearly see my purple top, along with the beginning of two bulges I've been trying to hide under baggy clothes for the last six months but it's been harder to do in the summer. I notice Katrina's shirt clings to her in almost the same way and for once I fight the urge to throw my arms across my chest.

Katrina spots my shoes. "You have the blue ones. What size?"

"Seven," I say, waiting for her to laugh. Mom thinks I'll end up being a size nine or so by the time my feet have finished growing.

"Me too," she says. "Want to trade? Just until tomorrow. Okay?"

I nod, still surprised, as we sit on the edge of her bed. It's not as big as my new one, but she has a yellow quilt for a comforter and at least six different pillows. We make the exchange, extending our feet to compare. Her shoes feel just right until I stand up and realize her feet are just slightly thinner than my own. But I don't say a word, and if my shoes feel too wide on her, she's not saying. We've made an agreement. We have an understanding.

"Emma, it's time to go home now," Mom yells up the stairs in the same delicate way Mrs. Liza Krause did earlier.

Right before I walk out, Katrina says, "Wait," and grabs one of the lip glosses off her dresser.

"Try it tomorrow," she says. "Berry Bouquet. I think it's perfect for you."

★ ★ ★ ★ ★

The next morning, I wait for Katrina out front where we first met, my banana-seat bike leaning nearby on its kickstand. I close my eyes but it's so sunny my lids turn everything a hazy yellow instead of black. I spread my arms and legs and move them back and forth as if I'm making a snow angel, marking my territory.

The movers have come back with one last load, and I hear Mom pleading with them, "Be careful with that. It's fragile. Everything in there is fragile."

The sunny space between my eyelids goes dark, like there's a cloud passing overhead. But when I open my eyes, it's Katrina standing above me. She reaches down to pull me up off the ground. A halo of light shines behind her head and as I grab her hand with my own, I wonder if she might be one of the angels I just made.

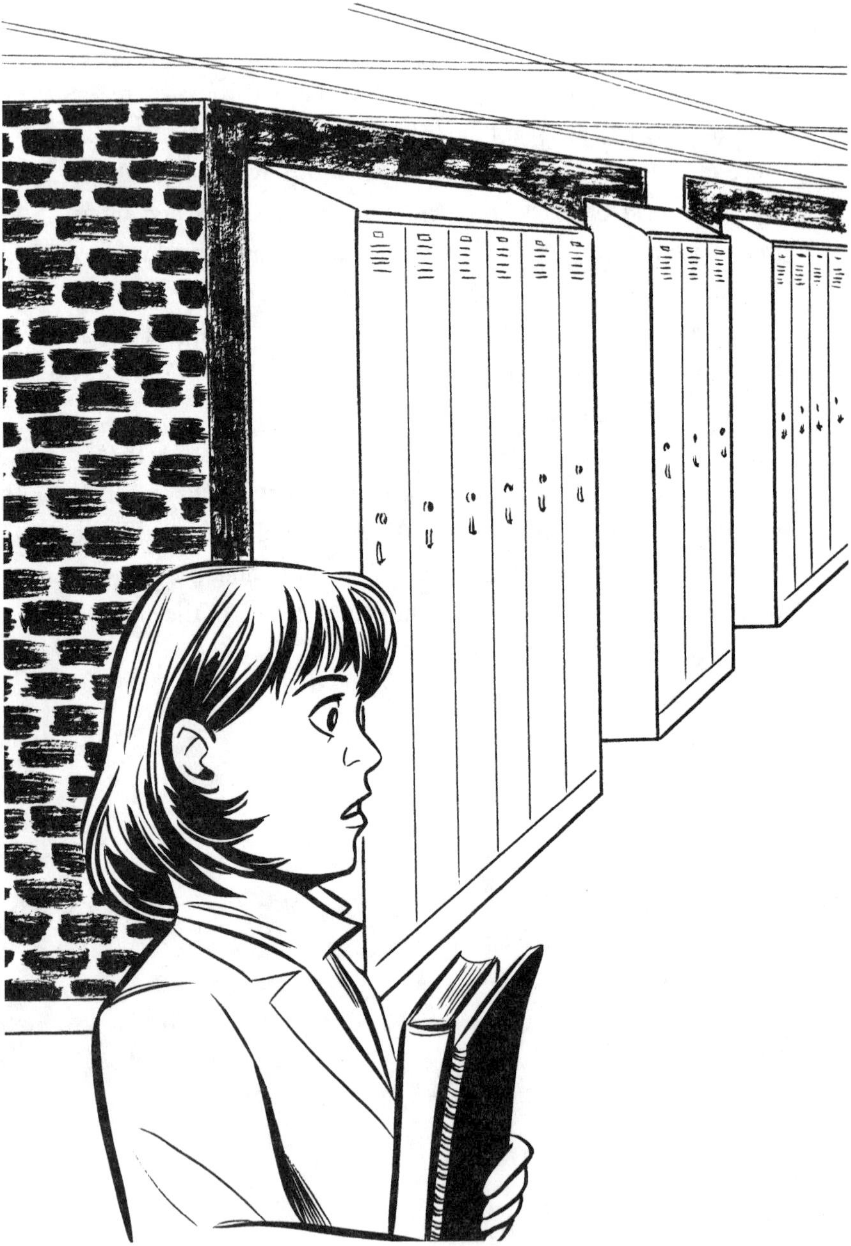

2

The Battle of Brownell

I am drafted, deployed to Brownell Middle School, and wounded within three days. The hit comes just after the last bell rings at three-fifteen P.M. I am walking down the stairway that curves around to the main lobby. My face is buried in a note Katrina passed to me before I walked into science, with Mr. Mariaki (who made it clear in no uncertain terms that he'd read any intercepted note out loud).

"Emma, you are SO lucky that you don't have Miss Cabott for English. She is SO boring. I can barely keep my eyes open. Zzzzzz. I can't believe I have nine more months of this. How will I survive?"

While I concentrate on my first official note from my new best friend, I'm oblivious to the approach of a brigade of sixth-grade boys led by Brian Van Eden. I've been at Brownell less than a week but Katrina has already tipped me off to his rank and file: you cannot get any higher. At first, I don't even realize he's talking to me. He never has before. But when I don't respond, he blocks my path, demanding my attention, his brown eyes two smug soldiers that never seem to flinch.

"Will you go with me?" he asks again.

But what I hear is "Will *you* go with me?," as if nobody else will help him on his mysterious journey. And before I can think about it any further, I answer what I think is a geography question.

"Where?"

It's just one word.

The boys pause for a second. Nobody rejects an offer like that from Brian Van Eden. When they realize that I didn't say no, that I just simply don't know what the hell they're talking about, that I am, oh God, uncool, the laughter is sharp and long as they scatter down the hallway to get as far from me as possible.

I'm still standing in the same spot when Katrina finds me five minutes later, the school now completely empty except for the janitor with his cleaning cart, sprinkling powdered soap on the linoleum floor.

"Where have you been?" she asks, chewing on a piece of red licorice. "We were supposed to meet by the bike racks." She's not mad, she's just stating the facts. "You want one?" she says, offering me the open pack. I never refuse candy unless it has coconut in it.

She lowers her voice immediately. "What happened?"

"It's bad," I manage, the first words out of my mouth since my fatal *Where?*

"How bad?" Katrina says.

I shake my head.

She changes her line of questioning. "Okay. Who?"

"Brian."

"Brian Van Eden?" she says in a high-pitched whisper, like how my aunt Carol talked about "the cancer" before Grandpa died.

It's like I have "the cancer."

It's like I'm dead.

* * * * *

"You said, 'Where?'"

Brian Van Eden's best friend, Tim Osborne, is in four of my six classes. The day after the incident, he begins with me during the homeroom announcements. In fifth-period math, he's still pursuing the issue while Mr. Houston scribbles formulas on the blackboard, his back turned to the class, chalk dust gathering on the edge of his hand.

"I said, 'What?,'" I tell him. It's the lie Katrina came up with.

We copy down the lesson on the board so we don't get caught talking.

$15 - x = 5$. *What is x?*

"No, you said, 'Where?' I was there. I heard you." He laughs.

$y + 11 = 13$. *What is y?*

"No, I didn't. I said 'What?' I didn't hear what Brian asked."

$x - y = Where.$

$x + y = What.$

The solution to this problem will remain unsolved for the next three years.

* * * * *

I should have known better. After all, I'd had almost three weeks of training.

Katrina and I had spent the last days of summer riding our bikes around town, from the moment we were released from our morning chores until we could see the fireflies. I quickly learned the lay of the land. Jacobson's department store was in the Village but the Over the Rainbow ice-cream shop was in the Hill. Schettler's drugstore was the easiest for stealing lipstick but Perry's had a better selection. Some days, we'd ride to the city pool and from our towels she'd point out, like numbers on a watch, other operatives.

"Three o'clock. Stephanie DeMarco. Total bitch. Dad owns the DeMarco Italian Restaurant chain. Personally, I think that's the only reason anyone is nice to her.

"Seven o'clock. Steve Moran. Leader of the nerds. See how pale his skin is? He's probably been inside for most of the summer, working on some science project. I think his dad is a big-time engineer for Ford. They live on Lakeshore," Katrina reports. It's the richest street in town. "Don't be fooled by the address. He's poison.

"Ten o'clock. Brian Van Eden. Don't turn your head until I tell you . . . hold on . . . okay, now," Katrina orders. There's a boy preparing to launch himself off the diving board. His body is a stretched piece of caramel, hair bleached out from the sun, stiff as straw from too much chlorine. Behind him, his cluster of male followers stand in breathless formation until their captain takes flight.

"He's it," Katrina whispers. "He's untouchable."

In my three weeks of Brownell boot-camp training, I've lost five pounds just from our daily bike rides. For the first time ever, I was actually excited about back-to-school shopping and Mom even said I could bring Katrina along. The Saturday of Labor Day weekend, we headed out at eight-thirty A.M. to East-land Mall, full from our pre-shopping breakfast of crumble-top apple muffins and orange juice without pulp.

Katrina came into the dressing room with me but I made Mom stand outside and wait. We'd make our initial assessment, then Katrina would talk up the favored items, trying to convince my mother that she was actually getting better deals and more bang for her buck.

"If you get the purple sweater, you can wear it with the Guess? jeans AND the black corduroy skirt."

"I saw that same jacket in *Seventeen* but it was fifty dollars more! What a deal!"

"Don't forget, you have to wear your tennis shoes in gym class three times a week, so you don't want them to wear out. These K-Swiss lasted me the entire year in fifth grade."

I walked out with new clothes enough for seven outfits, twelve counting pieces incorporated from Katrina's closet.

Even in full-dress uniform, there wasn't much I could do about my face. Katrina didn't have the same problem. She ate mostly healthy food and drank at least eight glasses of water a day, often munching on an apple or a plum, the purple-red juice staining her fingertips. Her skin glowed, but my forehead and chin sprouted a crop of blackheads on a regular basis, as if I had poured fertilizer on my face to help them grow. Sometimes my mother would suggest a warm washcloth or that I hover over a pot of hot water with a towel covering my head to trap the steam and open my pores. Usually this conversation ended with me locked in the bathroom crying while my mother stood outside explaining that she was only trying to help.

The night before the first day of school, I lined up all my weapons: gold hoop earrings, Love's Baby Soft perfume, Passion Pink polish.

My backpack said "Le Sportsac" like it was supposed to.

I carried a Trapper Keeper.

I was prepared.

I should have known better. But I had forgotten the most important rule of engagement: it's not what you say, but what you don't.

★ ★ ★ ★ ★

Word spreads fast of my defeat at the hands of Brian Van Eden. Even though no one buys it, I stick with my story.

"I said 'What?,' not 'Where.'"

I repeat this statement whenever the incident comes up, like I'm one of those carnival machines.

"I said 'What?,' not 'Where.'"

Fortunes Told, 25 cents, spitting out the same forecast every time.

"I said 'What?,' not 'Where.'"

I soon realize that I need to focus on not just what comes out of my mouth, but what I put into it. My body serves as a constant reminder. Its shape and form is clearly female, a prime target for the ammunition fired from the boys on a daily basis. Every morning after my shower I wrap myself in a terry-cloth towel and undergo sixteen or seventeen minutes of self-evaluation. The mirror reveals how the width of my legs and arms compare with the narrowness of my waist or the fullness of my breasts. I hold them in my hands and try to push them back into my chest. Mom's been sneaking glances at me lately too so I think she knows. Anytime I catch her, I try to hunch over a little bit or blouse my shirt out, but I can feel her eyes on me whenever I practice my piano lessons or push the grocery cart at Kroger's.

Every morning ends the same. By the time my mother yells upstairs that my eggs are getting cold, my eyes are squinting to make everything smaller, my brow wrinkled in disgust. I hide my development with my father's sweatshirts. Lucky for me, the style this year is loose and baggy, and I might be able to do what seems most important: blend in with everyone else.

"Emma!" Mom yells for the third time from the bottom of the stairs. "Your eggs!"

Eggs. Jesus. Stop feeding me, I think.

Just stop.

* * * * *

If I can't control what she gives me at home, I'll control what I take in at school. The ritual for lunch is established quickly. First, before entering the cafeteria, dump anything provided by my mother into the trash can in the girls' bathroom. I offer a silent apology to God because I know about the children starving in Africa . . . but nobody brown bags it—except for the math dorks.

Second, Katrina and I pool our allowances to buy a lemon-lime soda from the tabletop refrigerator with a glass door. Then we ask the lunch lady for one order of French fries, the small size, and place both items on our brown plastic tray.

The ultimate rule: if any boy comes into sight or—God forbid—sits down at our table while we are picking out greasy, salted fries one by one from the white paper bag, one of us immediately gets up and dumps the tray in the trash.

Boys or no boys, we do not finish the entire bag of fries. Ever.

* * * * *

The surprise attack comes after our dinner of baked chicken, corn on the cob, and white sticky rice. It's my turn to help Mom clear the plates. We are alone in the kitchen, the dish towel perched on her right shoulder as the disposal gargles our leftovers.

"I was thinking," Mom begins. "I was thinking, Emma, next week when your father goes to the Chicago auto show, we could go shopping."

"Again?" I ask. "But I just bought all my school clothes a few months ago. Is it for Christmas? Like an early present?" I hand her the salad bowl to dry.

"Mm, sort of. I was thinking it might be fun for us to go to the Jacobson's intimate apparel department. You know, just to see. It seems like you might be . . . ready . . . for that."

Boom!

The first shot is fired across my bow. I mean chest.

The Battle of Emma's Hills has begun.

* * * * *

The journey into enemy territory, "intimate apparel," second floor, is nothing like my last shopping trip. I have no weapons, no sisters in arms, just a general marching me to my fate. Mom approaches the salesclerk, a stout elderly woman with hair held in tight silver curls close to her head and coral lipstick bleeding and feathering at the corners of her mouth. She smells like rosewater. She smells like church. Her name badge reads "Mabel."

"Can I help you?" she asks, a tape measure around her neck like a stethoscope.

"Yes. We're looking for a bra for my daughter," Mom says. I keep surveillance in case anyone from school shows up.

"First time?" Mabel asks, giving us a nod as though our parakeet just died. "Come with me. Let's get you measured first."

I want to evaporate.

Mabel leads me to a dressing room in the back, the fluorescent lights overhead taunting me with their buzz. Mom tries to follow us into the dressing room but luckily there's no way the three of us can fit in there, so it's just me and Mabel. "You're going to have to take your shirt off for me to get a proper measurement." I hesitate. "Oh, don't worry, honey. I do this every day. There's no need to be shy."

"Emma, would you please cooperate?" Mom yells over the door. I'll do anything if she'll just shut up, so I pull my St. Paul's gray hooded sweatshirt over my head in one fast motion.

Mabel reaches around my rib cage with the tape, humming something that sounds like a show tune, turning me gently this way and that, lifting my arms into a defense stance. Then she makes little clucking sounds with her tongue and says, "Okey-dokey! Be right back," slipping out the door.

I try to make out what Mabel is saying to my mother but it's just a series of shuffles and murmurs. I stand alone in the dressing room, my arms over my chest, waiting. My skin looks

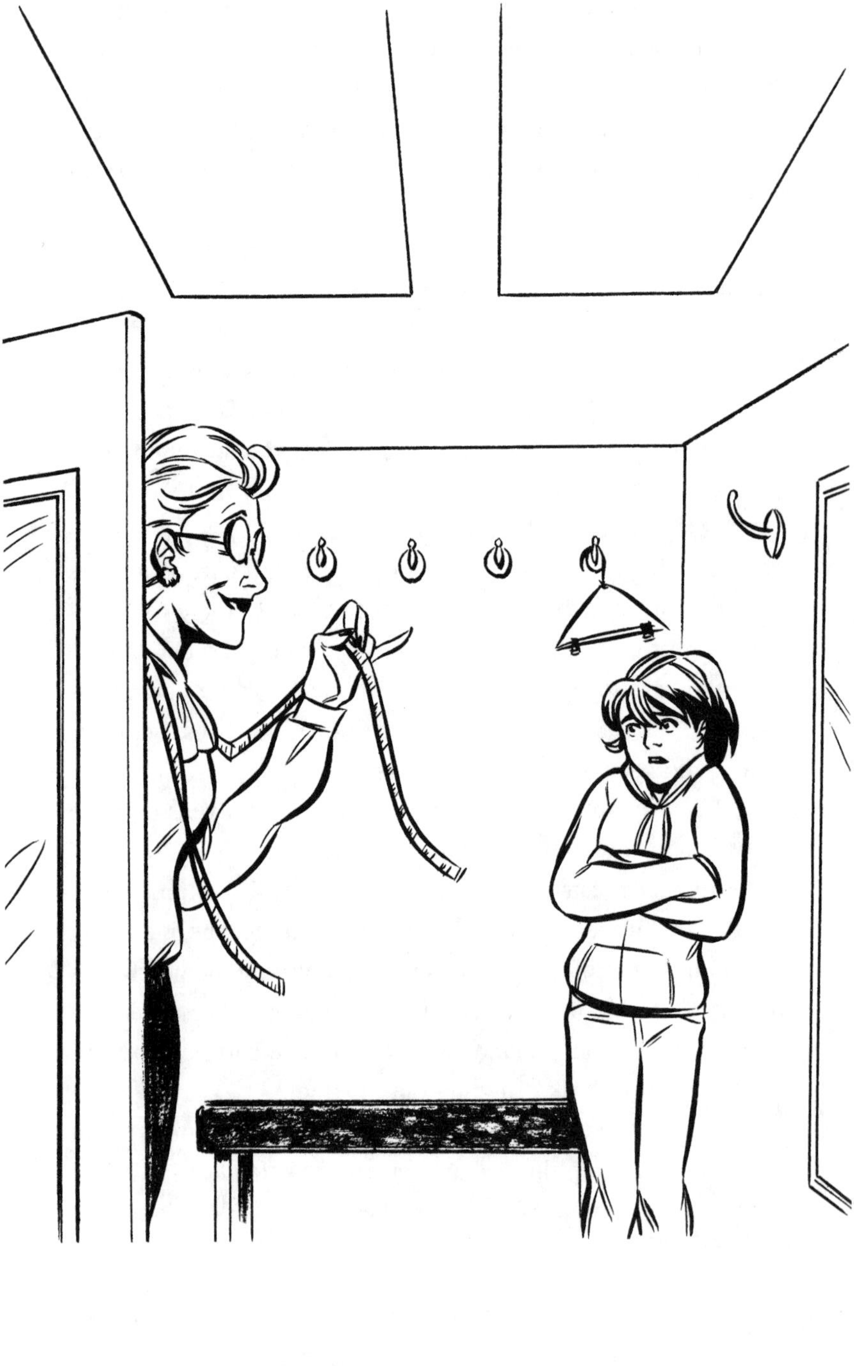

almost green under this light. My hair is messy from removing my shirt so quickly. My bangs need to be cut. I wonder if I should get a perm like Stephanie DeMarco.

"Try these!" I hear Mabel say from the other side of the door as her hand, holding a series of hangers, comes over the top. The bras flutter above me, peaches and nudes, lace and bows, eye hooks and straps.

I grab the little nooses and surrender.

★ ★ ★ ★ ★

My last defense is to try to avoid revealing too much. Gym class proves to be the greatest challenge. Brownell has one large gym that can be broken down into two smaller ones with a partition that folds like an accordion into the wall. The sixth-grade classes are held in the gym area farthest from the girls' locker room. We have exactly nine minutes to change from our clothes into our uniforms of reversible shirts—navy on one side, white on the other—and matching blue shorts that hit midthigh. Our locker room is a battleground where strategy and timing play a crucial role, and revealing the wrong information could mean severe penalties. For example, wearing a bra in sixth grade is a secret I keep by learning to put on my gym shirt without ever taking off my regular shirt first. It's a complicated procedure that involves putting my gym shirt on over my regular shirt and then slipping the regular shirt off underneath the protective shield.

I've got it down to fourteen seconds from start to finish.

By eighth grade, it's not only acceptable but also mandatory to parade around in your bra, waiting until the last possible minute to cover up to make sure everyone can see what you've got. I know this because there's an eighth-grade class that changes at the same time we do, and I try to scout their movements without being detected. I am counting down the days until I am free to expose what my mother finally made me get, what's really underneath this shirt, the stretch of flesh-colored fabric strangling me.

"Fool," it says to me. "Sooner or later, they're all going to know."

Six hundred and seventy-four more days to go.

The eighth-grade teacher is a woman with spiky black hair like the bottom of golf shoes. She always seems to be posing with some healthy food item, like she thinks she's in a sports ad—a granola bar, a carton of lemon yogurt, a banana. The sixth- and seventh-graders are assigned to a gruff beast we secretly call Sarge. His uniform never varies. He wears a tight, white, short-sleeved polo shirt with the collar open, exposing a broad chest of old, tanned, taut skin carpeted with curly, silvering hair. If we're lucky, his legs are covered with long, gray cotton pants. If we're not, he's wearing the shorts with an elastic band. His eyes leer behind oversize gold-rimmed, amber-tinted glasses. Salt-and-pepper hair and a matching mustache complete the look. And he is never without the silver whistle, freshly polished and dangling from a blue cord knotted at the back of his neck.

Sarge operates from the gym area near the boys' locker room, which is also right by his office. We've all heard the rumors about how he keeps his blinds open when the boys change after class, but these statements have never been verified. Every teacher at Brownell takes their turn and, right now, lucky for Sarge, people are more interested in the stories of the Spanish teacher changing her clothes three times a day in the broom closet of her classroom.

In Sarge's side of the gym is the stage used for school assemblies, where we chant in unison "Just Say NO!" to please the drug counselor who does not realize his fly is open. Sarge uses the stage as a place to exile the sit-outs. Sarge is a war veteran, Korean, I think, which to most of us seems like a far-off and distant battle. Casts on our arms or legs are a far cry from the actual war wounds he and his platoon endured, and our suffering fails to elicit a shred of his compassion.

The swimming unit proves to be an entirely new challenge. Swimming. Bathing suits. My shirt-switch routine won't work, and I realize I'll have to come up with a different strategy. The unit always hits in the first few weeks of spring. It is early enough so our bodies are still winter white. There are exceptions: the kids who are whisked away to their parents' time shares on Siesta Key over the holidays or the ones who are allowed to maintain their tans at the local salon on Mack Avenue, children who are barely twelve years old. Katrina and I spread urban legends about the girl whose insides got fried after four visits.

We are pasty and bitter.

I execute my plan carefully, making sure my cramps begin the Friday before swim week. It gives credibility to the timing when I turn in the forged note from my mother on Monday morning. For swim week, we're allowed a few extra minutes to change into the school-issued suits. We can wear our own underwear underneath if we want, but of course none of the girls will risk the extra padding. The male suits are embarrassing—racing style, in blue or black—but the boys make a joke of it, led by

Brian Van Eden of course, who makes beat-box noises while strutting around the pool deck like John Travolta.

The suits we girls are forced to wear are one piece, the bottoms cut low on our hips, the necklines high and respectable. The fashion is dated but bearable. It is the sizing that haunts us, the suits color coded and labeled on the outside for all to see. This is another reason I fake a week-long period. By sixth grade, I no longer fit into the cool size, black. I've become a blue.

A big, fat blue.

Chapter 3

War Memorial Dances

At 6:47 P.M., Katrina and I split the last piece of the small cheese pizza delivered from the Little Caesar's, trying to decide if we will wear Mulberry Stain or Peaches 'n' Cream lip gloss. Manners forgotten and mouth full, one of the tubes becomes my mike for lip-synching Debbie Gibson songs to the mirror. I grab Katrina's black floppy hat from the top of her lampshade and tilt the brim over my eyes, wishing I were blond and sixteen and writing hit pop songs. In the reflection I see Katrina wander back to her closet for the fifth time in as many minutes, eyeing possible replacements for the white frilly blouse she is currently wearing.

In thirty-one minutes, we will load into the Krauses' blue station wagon, and her father will drop us off at the Grosse

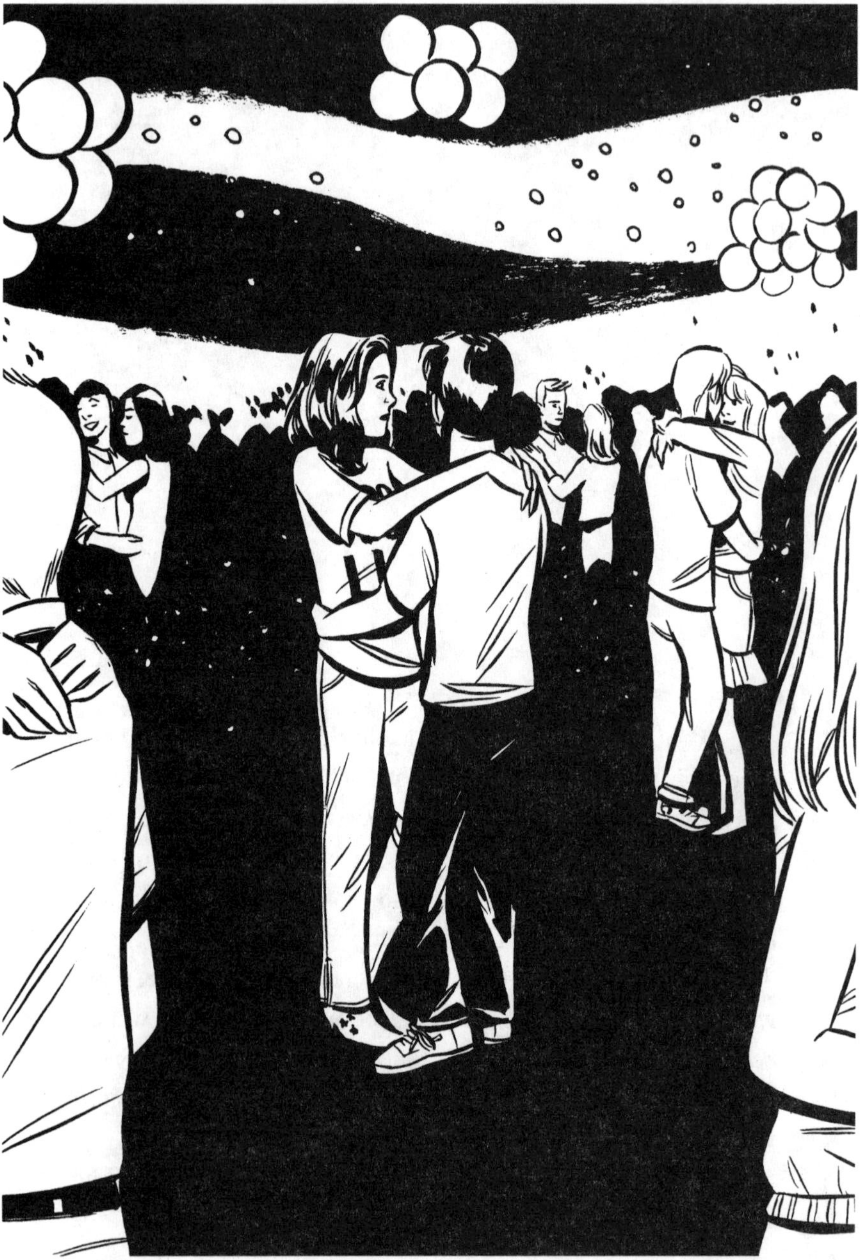

Pointe War Memorial, an Italian Renaissance–style home that hugs Lake St. Clair. The once private estate has now been transformed into a community center where dances are held once a month for the sixth-, seventh-, and eighth-graders of Grosse Pointe. Public and private schools are eligible as long as they are within the city limits, of course.

Every dance has a theme. It's March, so with nothing obvious to go to like Fourth of July or Valentine's Day, the planners settled on the "Winter White" dance. I have chosen my white Guess? jeans with zippers at the bottom, short white boots studded with silver stars, bought with money from Christmas, and a white T-shirt with the words "Choose Life" silk-screened on the front in giant black block letters, just like the one from the Wham! video. Katrina says that now that the cute one with the golden hair is making a solo album, they'll never get back together, but I refuse to believe it.

"Stop fussing!" I tell her, adding more of the blue glitter left over from Halloween to my eyelids. "You look great." Katrina makes a face, pulling at the front of her blouse. "You look just like Prince!" Her eyes brighten. "You know, Debbie Gibson wore a shirt like that in her last video too." She walks away from the mirror, satisfied.

Tonight is crucial for both of us. Our crushes are best friends, two boys who wear flannel shirts tied around their waists, skateboarding, before and after school, by the bike racks. I share art class with mine, third period, and we have been passing notes trying to set up our two respective friends. We spread out the evidence on Katrina's bedroom floor, examining his messy boyish writing, rereading the declarations.

"Hey. What's up? I don't know what to paint. This is so lame. Anyway, I told Chris he should ask Katrina and he said he was thinking

about it. Make sure you are at the dance by 8 or they won't let you in. We'll meet U inside. What R U wearing? Bye!"

Earlier in the week, he started including pictures of heavy-metal bands into my notes, adding the P.S., "Who is your favorite?"

When I wrote back my answer, he responded, "Mine too."

He thinks we worship the same God.

We take these things as signs of hope.

★ ★ ★ ★ ★

At 7:49 P.M., we make our entrance into the lobby of the ballroom. Our coats have been off since we got out of the car and rounded the corner, out of sight of Mr. Krause, who insisted we wear them because of our light cotton shirts, bare necks and arms, and the thirty-four-degree air destined to bring strep throat and flu. We hand the coats to the parent chaperone, who hangs them on the mobile silver racks with the others, and shove our claim tickets into our pockets, anxious to escape the bright lights so cruel to our thirteen-year-old imperfections.

"Do you see them?" Katrina whispers to me, and I shake my head no, pulling her arm and leading her through the doorway and toward the dance floor. It is a large room, the north wall a series of floor-to-ceiling windows, the shades drawn to enhance the black lights placed in all four corners. Every speck of white glows, our bodies victims of radiation exposure, eyes and teeth brief toxic flashes. Those rebels in all black try to fade into the walls, but the small pieces of lint on their garb reflect their location and contempt.

A DJ is set up on the far end of the room, sheltered in a maze of folding tables and equipment, milk crates of records and a large disco ball twirling above his head. The girls gather in small clusters, whispering in each other's ears and clearly segregated from the boys, who are racing through the room, roughhousing and trying not to get caught. It is far too early to be dancing and the DJ knows this, saving the classic "Rock Lobster" for later.

While I am trying to act like I am not looking for anyone in particular, a pair of hands comes up around my face, covering my eyes. When I feel them with my own, I find long, broad fingers and scrapes that must have come from a fall on the homebuilt half pipe.

"Guess who?"

I shrug my shoulders at the falsetto and giggle. The boys we like are standing right behind us, and mine asks if I will help bring back pop for everyone. I take the hint and mouth "I told you" to Katrina before walking out the side door.

My crush pulls out a turquoise-green wallet with a Velcro tab and asks what I want. I roll my eyes and say, "Diet, of course!" He hands over a few dollar bills and gets four small Styrofoam cups in return, two diets and two regulars, and we go to an empty couch in the lobby to wait, as drinks are not allowed inside. He is wearing regular denim jeans and a white T-shirt with a picture of Mötley Crüe on the front.

"Nice WHITE outfit," I tease.

"Hey, it's white! See?" And he points to his sleeves and collar. I laugh and tug on my large silver hoop earring.

"So, what's the deal? Is he asking her or what?"

"You'll see, you'll see." As soon as it's said, Katrina and Chris enter the lobby holding hands and I know the deal is done. We hand them their drinks to celebrate.

Everyone agrees that the dance is lame except for the black

lights, and we hear the beginnings of the first slow song. Katrina and Chris go in for their inaugural dance as a couple, and this will serve as "their song." We squeeze hands before she leaves because it is a good one, "With or Without You," by U2. My crush and I stand near the doorway, watching the other two try to find a dark corner away from the circulating chaperones so they can get in a few minutes of making out.

Slow songs can be the most incredible or the most awkward time. If I am going with someone, this is the moment to shine and show it off, arms circled around his neck, his around my waist. If not, I linger with the other single girls for the first minute of the song, holding my breath for the passage of the boys with scanning eyes. If I don't feel the tap on my shoulder before the song reaches the first chorus, I dash for the bathroom, and take extra time at the mirror fixing my eyeliner, trying to forget that no one asked me to dance.

The DJ usually plays two slow songs in a row, and at the beginning of the second one, "Could've Been," by Tiffany, my crush grabs my hand and says, "Let's go spy." He pulls me close to him and I can smell the cologne he must have borrowed from his older brother. It is crisp and woodsy, and my chin rests between his shoulder and neck.

I wonder if he can tell I am wearing my bra.

We position ourselves within arm's length of Katrina and Chris, turning in slow circles so the boys face each other at the same time. I know they are exchanging signals, but then again, Katrina and I are doing the same, my eyes open wide, brows raised, and she knows what I am trying to figure out. Is he dancing with me just to tease his friend or does he like me too? Before she can send me a sign, we rotate, and when I come around facing her again, her lips are locked with Chris's, the tips of their tongues toasting their union.

★ ★ ★ ★ ★

At 9:47 P.M., I'm on my third diet pop, Katrina's shirt is wrinkled, and after jumping up and down during "Shout," my blue eye glitter is melted and gone. I am no closer to an answer. My crush has danced with me a handful of times but made only small talk throughout most of the songs, pointing out what I can't see behind me.

"Brian Van Eden has his hands on Stephanie DeMarco's ass!"

I think, Yeah, well, follow the leader, but he just sings along with Whitesnake.

Katrina separates herself from her newfound love for a few minutes to join me in the bathroom, where ten other girls gather around two small sinks, all trying to craft plans to snag boys before the evening slips to a state of emergency: the final slow song of the night. We huddle by the brown-paper-towel dispenser to review.

"We only danced together three times, and once was to spy on you."

"Yes, but he hasn't asked anyone else to dance ALL night."

"But he WAS talking to that girl, what's-her-name, with the long blond hair, from St. Clare."

"Yes, but their families are friends. Chris told me. They're like cousins."

"Did you tell him I liked him?"

"NO! No. But . . ."

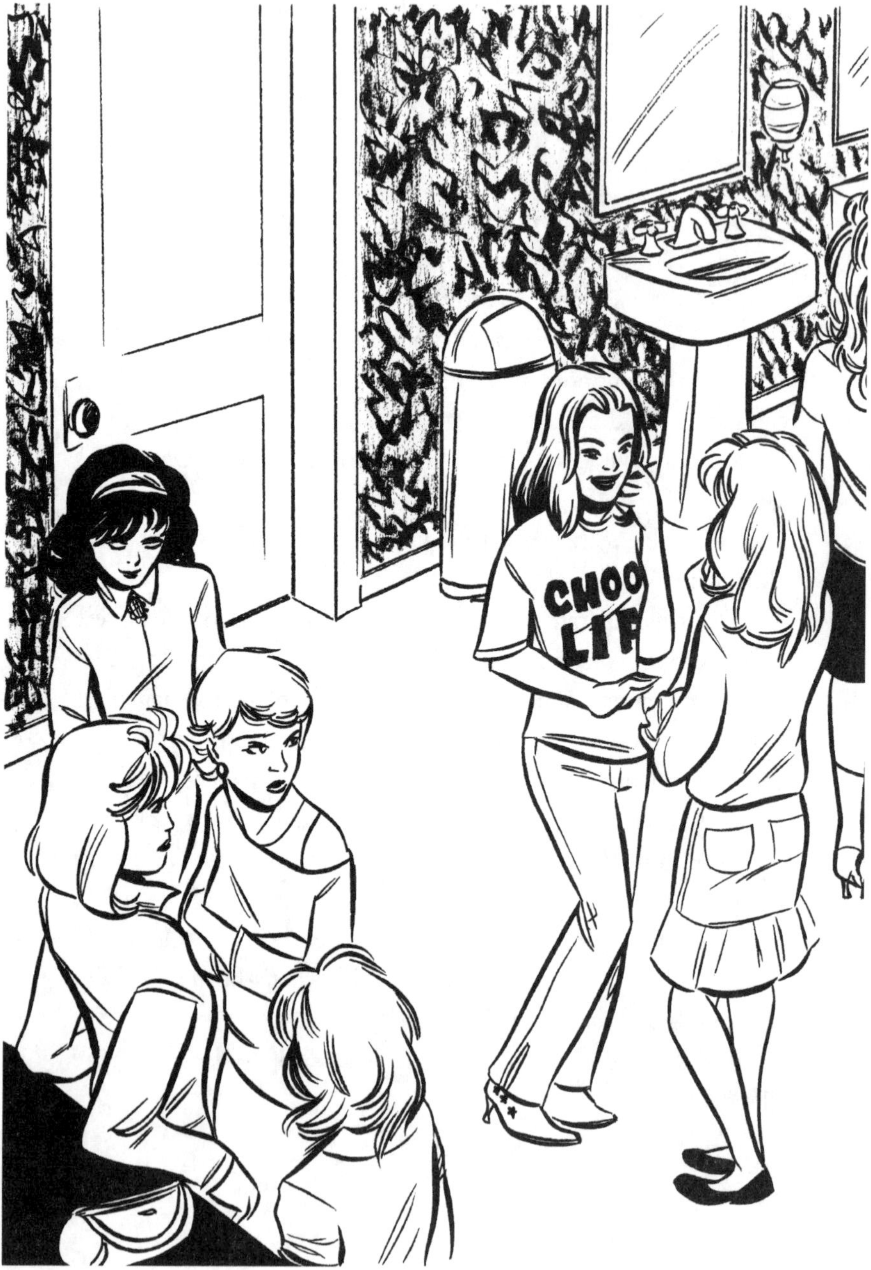
CHOO
LIP

"But what?"

"He asked me if you did."

My squeal earns me a dirty look from the other Geneva conferences. I lower my voice and continue.

"WHAT did you SAY?"

"I said I didn't know and I would ask."

"Is that what he thinks you're doing right now?"

"Probably." We move on to strategy. "Look, you've got to dance the last slow song with him. Whatever you've got to do to make that happen, do it. He's shy."

"No he's not!" I pause. "Do you really think he is?"

"Yes. So just pretend you want to spy on us again." I hand her my lip gloss as she doles out the Velamints before we exit the bathroom.

Katrina's hand immediately goes back to Chris's while my crush and I eye each other nervously. We all know what has been discussed. His bangs are a bit damp against his forehead. My instinct is to reach out and push them back, and I do. His head jerks up, and I am wondering if I have just blown it when I hear the DJ say, "All right, all you lovebirds out there! This is the LAST slow song of the night, so if you've been wanting to get out here, this is your LAST chance!"

Katrina and Chris dart out onto the congested dance floor with the other fireflies. It's not just any last slow song, it's an oldie but a goodie, "Purple Rain," by Prince. It is eight minutes and forty-five seconds long. It is a key element in the sound track of the life I fantasize about with him. When the song reaches the point where violins seem to swell with ache, my crush will no longer be able to contain his feelings for me. While the others on the dance floor look on with awe and jealousy, he will kiss me, long and deep, cupping the bottom of my chin with his hand. I have played this exact scene in my head on a nightly basis, falling asleep with the cassette running in my tape deck.

My crush's hand is nowhere near my chin; it has not left his forehead since I touched it. He presses his fingers against the spot like he has a headache. I take a deep breath and Katrina's advice and say, "So. Should we go spy again?" I concentrate on his mouth, hoping his lips will form the beginning of a yes, and notice that he still has braces on his bottom teeth.

"Let's—" He stops midsentence, eyes switching focus from me to beyond me. Then I feel the tap on my shoulder and turn around to find one of the other sixth-graders standing in front of me. I think his name is Rob, but it could be Bob. He has dark hair black as oil and is scratching the back of his head when he says, voice shaking, "Do you want to dance?"

Before I can answer, without even looking back, I know that my crush, sleeves and collar sufficient camouflage, has disappeared into the glowing, stark-white night.

Chapter 4

Season's Greetings

In Grosse Pointe, to ski is to survive. This becomes clear two days before Thanksgiving break when Katrina says to me, "Did you hear what happened with Mike Cleveland and Stephanie DeMarco over the weekend?"

Of course I did, but I know the second I discuss it with Katrina, it becomes fact instead of fable. The breaking news is that Stephanie DeMarco has dumped Brian Van Eden and is now officially going with Mike Cleveland—my Mike Cleveland. Well, not mine yet, but he would've been. I've been working on him for three months, including the Winter White War Memorial dance, several notes passed to his best friend, and a shared math class with Mike himself. He told me he wanted to be a pediatrician.

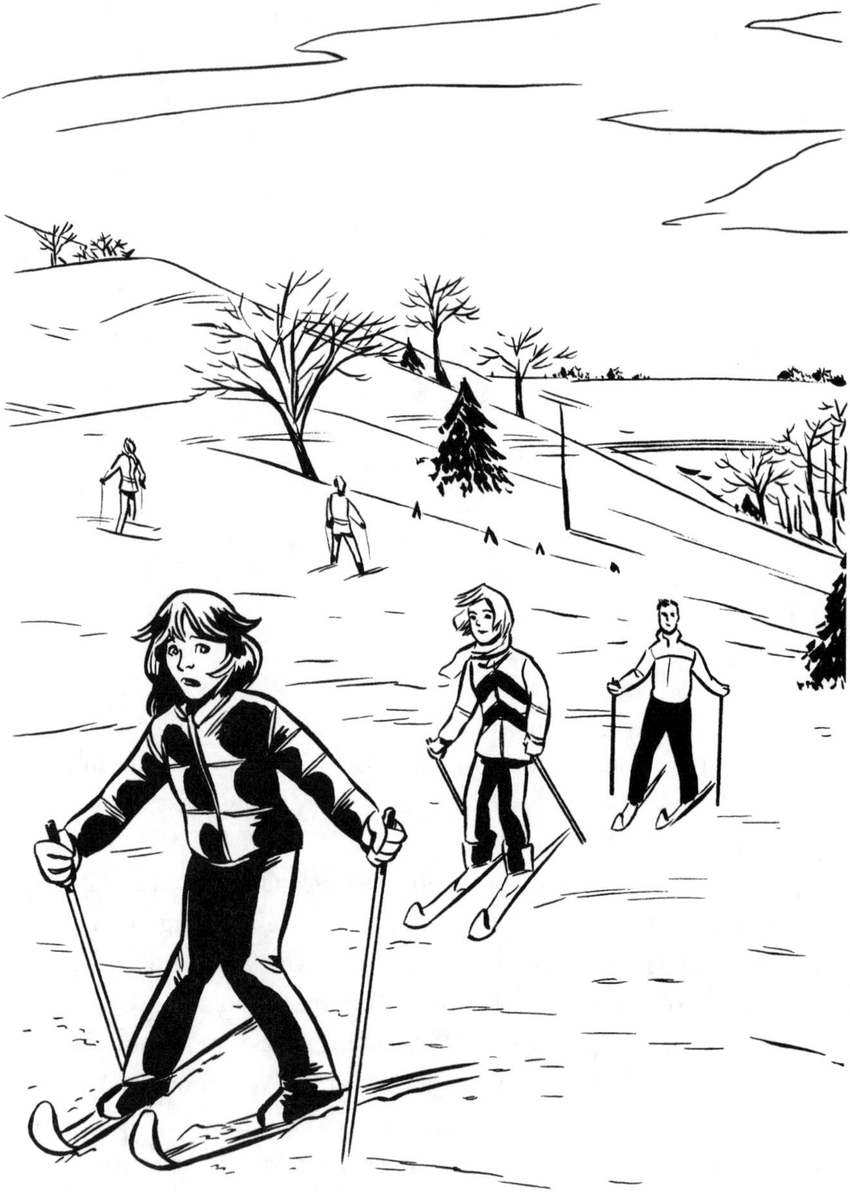

I thought we had something.

Their romance apparently blossomed over the weekend during a Blizzards Ski Club trip. If I don't join now, I'll spend the next ten Monday mornings hearing about how Mike sat with Stephanie in the back of the bus; how he bought her hot chocolate from the lodge; how they made out on the chair lift; and eventually how he told her he loved her in the middle of a snowball fight. Then they'll probably date all through high school and go to the same college and get married and tell their kids how they got together on the slopes, all because I never learned how.

Most weekends, the club ends up going to one of three locations, all within an hour-and-a-half drive from Grosse Pointe: Pine Knob, Mount Brighton, or Mount Holly. None of these places are really mountains, just hills of trash that have been seeded with grass and covered in mostly manufactured snow.

Stephanie and Mike are sitting at the same table. She sips on a Capri Sun while he offers her half of his turkey sandwich. She declines but leans closer to whisper something in his ear. He laughs, flipping his black bangs from his eyes and shoving bits of bread into his mouth.

I can see the wedding invitations. The ceremony will be at St. Paul's Church on the Lake, the reception at the Grosse Pointe Yacht Club.

"I'm joining Blizzards."

"How?" Katrina asks, biting on her pinkie nail.

"Divorce," I tell her. "Divorce."

* * * * *

"So what do you think?"

It's Tuesday after school. I have just laid out to Mom my pitch for classes and skis. We're in the kitchen and I sit on a stool pulling silverware out of the drawer as she makes dinner.

She sighs. "How much money have you saved from baby-sitting?"

"Seventy-four dollars," I tell her. "But I wanted to use it to buy Christmas presents."

She sighs again as she places defrosted wet chicken in a glass baking pan, sprinkling seasoned bread crumbs over the top. When she finally gets to the "Why don't you ask your father?" part, I launch my prepared response.

"But I'm already going to ask him for the money for skis and boots and a jacket. All I want from you, as a Christmas present, is the money for club fees." As I tell her this, I realize I've once again pulled out four place settings when we now need only three.

"Don't you think skis and boots and a jacket is an awful lot to ask for for one Christmas?" Mom says, squeezing a lemon half over the dusted breasts.

I give her a look that says something like "Don't you think you two sort of owe me for completely screwing up my life with your stupid divorce?" but I say nothing.

She meets my eyes with her own, keeping quiet at first as she slides the chicken into the oven. The door closes as she tells me, "Set the table. I'll call your father after dinner."

Later that night, after a long, hushed phone call, Mom leans in the doorway of my bedroom while I work on my social studies report.

"We'll do it, for Christmas. But you'll have to wait until after the holidays for the skis and boots to go on sale." That means I'll have to rent for the next couple of Saturdays. And though she doesn't say it, I know my parents also want to send me on a few trips before actually purchasing the equipment. They are wary of my commitment, and with good reason. I've never played a team sport or been able to pull myself to the top of the ropes in gym class. I have no hand-eye coordination and I am unusually afraid of breaking my bones. But I'm also determined to prove to them that I'm serious.

"This is the greatest Christmas present ever," I tell Mom.

She smiles for the first time in about three months before she shuts my door while saying good night.

* * * * *

My ski coat cannot wait, so the next Thursday Dad pulls into our driveway after work and honks.

He doesn't come to the door anymore.

We ride to Schummer's Ski Shop on Mack Avenue where I try on seven different coats before deciding on a black one with pink-and-white trim. Even though it's not his usual night and my brother isn't with us, afterward Dad takes me to dinner at Big Boy's.

"I'll have the ribs with coleslaw, and a Coke," Dad tells the waitress. She's smacking a piece of green gum between her teeth. Her mascara is barely holding on.

"Okay, Frank. What about the little lady here?"

Frank?

Dad whistles along to the Muzak piped through the restaurant.

"I'll have the chicken parmigiana," I tell her, pointing to the picture on the menu, "and a Diet Coke."

"Hey, Kathy," Dad says to the waitress between tunes, "for dessert, why don't you add a piece of chocolate cake, the one with the cherries, and two forks?"

Kathy?

She takes our menus and drags her heavy black shoes like horse's hooves toward the kitchen.

"How does she know your name?"

"Oh, you know, I don't like to cook much," Dad says.

"Oh. Who else do you come here with?"

"No one. Just myself. I really like the quiet time, I catch up on my newspaper and my books and all that."

I nod, count to fifteen, excuse myself, and follow the sign that says "Rest Room." It's a single stall and I make sure to lock the door before sitting on the closed toilet seat, my face buried in my hands.

* * * * *

On the drive home, my belly is full but I feel no guilt because Dad is the one person who never keeps score when I eat. I hold my new coat in my lap. It feels soft, like the feather pillows on what is now just Mom's bed. The snow crunches below the car as it crawls into the frozen tire tracks. It's falling quickly enough to dust over the path so Dad turns on his favorite AM radio station for a news update.

"The I-94 overpass will be closed tonight due to hazardous ice. Continued snowfall is expected tomorrow night, with at least three or four inches before sunrise. Highs around twenty-nine degrees, lows around fourteen."

The forecast sounds perfect.

It is one of the only times I get everything I think I want

and need without too much of a struggle, and I wonder if this is what it feels like to always be a Grosse Pointe girl.

★ ★ ★ ★ ★

The morning of my first trip as a part of Blizzards, I show up at the drop-off location, a mansion in Grosse Pointe Park. A chartered bus is parked out front and quickly fills up with Blizzards members and equipment and of course several chaperones. Katrina joined last year and she meets me there, carrying her own set of skis that match her navy-blue-and-green coat.

"I wish I had my new skis already," I think out loud but Katrina shrugs off this detail.

"I bought mine used. That's practically like renting." She knots her red scarf. "Cool jacket."

"Thanks."

As I board the bus, I get a lot of questions, like "When did YOU join?" and "Where are your skis?," but most of the kids know my parents are getting divorced. That, with an occasional "I'm getting new skis for Christmas," seems to be enough for now.

We grab seats together as the bus pulls away. "You should take the beginners' class when you get there," Katrina says a little too loudly.

I shake my head. "What if someone sees me?" I've lowered my voice to a whisper, hoping she'll follow.

"Who cares? Everyone at some point had to take the beginners' class to get their first patch. Then you take the next one, then the next one. This is how it works."

Six rows back, Mike and Stephanie are blowing onto the windows of the bus. In the fog, Stephanie draws a smiley face. Mike adds a heart around it.

Katrina pulls me in closer.

"When you get to the top of the hill, just make a V with your skis. The point of the V should be headed toward the bottom of the hill. It'll slow you down."

These are good tips and I wonder if I should be taking notes.

"If you lose control and can't stop, fall to one side and make sure your poles don't hit your head. And stay on the bunny hills at first. These are the ones that use towropes to get to the top.

"Let me see your gloves," she adds, nodding with approval once she has inspected the palms.

"Good. They've got grips on them. Hold on tight to the rope and lean back, otherwise you won't be able to grab it and you'll fall and stop the line. Never stop the line."

I am wondering just what happens if you do stop the line and also what the hell I've gotten myself into, when Tim Osborne and Todd Anderson move into the empty seats behind us.

"Hey, Katrina," Tim says, drinking a Coke at 9:17 A.M. "Did you finish the social studies report yet?"

It's a mapping report, due on Monday. I know for a fact that Katrina finished it three days ago because I saw it sitting on her desk in her bedroom in a plastic cover with a blue bar. But it's not cool to be early, so she says, "I haven't even started yet."

"Me either. I'm screwed." Tim takes the last swig of his Coke and crunches the can against the side of the bus. Katrina laughs. Tim is pretty cute, but it's just a matter of time before he brings up the incident with Brian Van Eden, when Brian asked me to go with him and I said, "Where?"

Todd Anderson saves me with a diversion. "Have you ever skied before?"

"No, I probably suck," I say, trying to laugh and make it funny.

Then Todd says, "Well, it's sort of hard the first day or so, but then you get the hang of it," which is a super-nice thing to say and so of course I immediately start wondering if that means he sort of likes me. I'm wearing a white turtleneck underneath my coat and black snow pants over my jeans. All morning I've been thinking I look fat, but now, seeing everyone else on the bus, we all sort of look like puffy astronauts.

I smile at Todd while sucking in my cheeks and wonder if Mike Cleveland is watching.

Two more of Tim's Cokes and a shared bag of corn chips later, we finally arrive at this week's destination, Mount Brighton. As we exit the bus and some grab their gear, one of the supervisors hands us our passes, stickers wrapped around a wire piece bent into the shape of a triangle, then attached to our coat zippers. The trick is to keep the badges, accumulating them trip after trip, as long as they'll withstand the weather. These passes are a testament of how much we can endure.

I walk to the rental shack with $30 in my pocket, enough to cover equipment fees and lunch. Even though I tell him my shoe size, the guy at the counter takes a measurement of my foot and disappears into the racks. A few minutes later, he returns with a pair of red boots and gray-and-red skis, which absolutely do not go with my outfit but it doesn't look like I have much choice.

The boots are hard plastic and I'm certain he's grabbed the wrong size until I finally shove my foot through to the bottom. The casing feels tight around my ankles and the skis seem much thinner now that they are below my feet. Once everything is on, it takes me about fifteen minutes to get from the bench in the rental shack to the holding area outside where Katrina waits for me, booted up and ready to go.

"How do they feel?" she asks.

"Um, okay," I lie, trying to be tough.

"Do you want to try this bunny hill first?" she says, motioning toward the closest one.

The towrope is only about twenty feet away but it might as well be in Wisconsin. With the third bar patch on her jacket, Katrina is well beyond the bunny hills, but I don't want to go alone so I accept her offer.

We make our way toward the line.

"Bend your knees," Katrina offers as a last-minute suggestion.

My legs are two steel beams, my knees petrified.

The kids in line seem like they've all been through this before. I try to merge but there's a bead of sweat trickling down my temple and I haven't even reached the top of the mountain yet. Katrina lets me go ahead of her, buffering my back end. I watch how the kids ahead of me negotiate the rope, how they tuck their poles under their arms and grab on, all in a matter of seconds.

When it's my turn, the first thing I do is drop both of my poles. The rope operator picks them up and slides them back under my arm.

It's like the entire school just witnessed my mom buttoning up my coat.

I try to grab the cord but can't get a solid grip. And though I've already committed the ultimate sin by stopping the line, the towrope waits for no one and burns through my hands as though I'm not even there.

"Grab tight!" the operator barks and I hear a few giggles

behind me and so I grab it, really grab it this time, and I jerk back a little bit at first but then I'm lifted off and moving and heading toward the summit.

* * * * *

By Christmas Eve, I've been on three trips with Blizzards, earned my yellow beginners' patch, and though I'm still on the bunny hills, I've even learned how to play downhill snow tag with the others at the end of the day.

This is the first year with a split holiday and the agreement is Mom's on Christmas Eve, Dad's on Christmas Day. At Mom's house, we went to the lot in St. Clair Shores to pick out a live tree, just like we do every year. We unwrapped our ornaments stored in the tissue-lined, white Lord & Taylor department-store boxes. The glittered pinecone and clothespin Rudolph ornaments I made in elementary school were both still there. It all seemed familiar and normal except for the fact that the only presents underneath our tree marked "To Dad" or "To Mom" were from me or Jack.

Mom's plan is to do the forty-five-minute drive to Grandma and Grandpa Martin's house for dinner. Mom's sister, Rachel, will be there too. Rachel is also divorced and has one kid, a girl named Katie. She's a couple of years younger than me, and mostly wants to play with her new Barbies or color, both of which we are way too old for. Jack never plays with me anymore anyway. He's a freshman now and spends most of the night sitting in Grandma's navy armchair in the living room, eating salted cashews and reading *Wolverine* comics.

Grandpa sits on the living-room couch with my brother and Katie, flipping between holiday specials on TV while I help my mom and Rachel and Grandma in the kitchen. My aunt Rachel has frosted blond hair and icy blue eyes, like Farrah Fawcett, and she's even modeled at the auto show and been in a few magazines. Her laugh is contagious, like a hiccup or a yawn, a strong, gasping laugh that comes from her belly. We wash carrots and peel potatoes and shred cheese while Aunt Rachel entertains us with stories from her real job as a nurse, mostly about how she tricks the kids into looking at teddy bears while she gives them their shots.

Dinner is served and I keep a close eye on my servings of gravy and butter pats for my rolls. Just like last year, there are three desserts to choose from, chocolate pudding with Cool Whip, apple-nut cobbler, and pumpkin pie because Grandpa doesn't like nuts and Grandma can't have chocolate.

Then we open presents. Mom buys our gifts for Grandma and Grandpa, a terry-cloth bathrobe for her and for him a fishing-tackle box. They give me a pair of black furry earmuffs.

"For your ski club," Grandma explains. I thank both of them but don't say that no one wears hats, let alone earmuffs.

Of course, I've got nothing to open from Mom, and as I watch Jack unwrap two Polo sweaters, a leather wallet, and a game for our Commodore computer, I'm sort of wishing I hadn't asked for all the ski stuff to be my Christmas present. But then Mom pulls from her purse a small gray-silver box with a pink bow.

"I thought you should have something to open," she says, smiling, and I can tell by the box that it's from the Jacobson's store in the Village. Inside are six rhinestone stack bracelets I pointed out a few weeks ago while we were picking up Grandma's robe. I love them, the way they clink against each other and shine on my wrist, so I give her a kiss and hand her our gifts. Jack and I combined funds so we could get her the bath set from Crabtree & Evelyn, the silver dangle earrings, and the silk, flowered scarf. This year, we figured she could use an extra present or two.

By the time we're done, Grandpa is already nodding off, so we pile into the car with trays of leftovers wrapped in foil and

Jack taking shotgun of course. I rest my head against the cold window in the backseat, staring at the Christmas lights in the trees and plastic Santas and glowing mangers on the lawns of the houses we drive by. Dad usually puts up our outdoor lights, a string of fat bulbs in all different colors, but this year they're still sitting untouched in a box in the basement.

I play with the bracelets on my wrist and close my eyes, trying to tune out the Christmas carols on the car radio because they always make me sad and these days, I never let anyone see me cry.

* * * * *

My parents told us on the Sunday after Easter. Mom said we needed to have a "family meeting" after dinner, that there was "important news."

I thought she might be pregnant.

After they delivered the true verdict, Jack developed a sudden case of bloodshot eyes and fled our house on his ten-speed.

Dad turned on *60 Minutes* and refreshed his drink, just like any other Sunday.

Mom took me to the drugstore. We bought fabric softener, laundry bleach, cold cream, three birthday cards for no one in particular, a can of black shoe polish, and gardening gloves.

"Pick out something you want," Mom said in the checkout line, motioning toward the rows of gum packs, hard candies, and chocolate bars.

I placed a roll of root beer LifeSavers on the belt, and swallowed every single one of them before we had even pulled back into our driveway.

Twenty minutes later, I threw up as soon as I saw Dad's suitcase on the bed. The tiny candy rings floated in the toilet water below me, waiting for someone to grab hold of them. There were no survivors.

* * * * *

Christmas morning, Mom drops us off at Dad's before breakfast. He's made pancakes and peppered bacon and freshly squeezed orange juice.

I ignore the pulp.

We eat before opening presents. Dad doesn't have a tree, just a lighted wreath above the mantel, so we stack our gifts near the fireplace in the duplex he's renting. Dad's got a secret extra present for me too, the new Cure tape, and I'm thinking Jack must have tipped him off because this is the same person who spelled INXS like "In Excess."

Jack and I couldn't agree on what to get Dad, so this time we did two separate presents. From Jack, Dad gets a big coffee-table book about Vietnam because he used to be in the army. From me, Dad gets a big coffee-table book about vintage cars because he also works in the auto industry. We play a few rounds of gin rummy at the breakfast table, pushing the dishes to one side to make room, until it's one o'clock and time to go to Dad's sister's house.

My aunt Betty lives in Grosse Pointe too, so it takes only about five minutes to get there. She's got three kids, all boys, all older, none of them interested in playing or makeup or games. At Betty's house, there's a football game on and the food is already on the table for people to pick at whenever they feel like it, mostly things like honey-baked hams and macaroni salad and cold cuts and pickles. The boys are all engrossed in the game.

I take a plate of crackers and cheese and a diet pop into the kitchen, sit at the Formica table, and flip through Aunt Betty's catalogs. The adults are allowed to smoke in this house, and some of the cigarettes are an unfamiliar brown instead of the usual white on the outside.

My stomach doesn't feel so good and I'm thinking I ate too many pancakes and definitely way too much bacon as I quietly head to the bathroom. I don't really feel like I'm going to throw up, but something is different.

When I sit down on the toilet, I don't even see it at first. I'm just sitting there waiting for something to happen and after a while nothing does, so I reach down to pull up my underwear and corduroys and see the stain. It's sort of a brownish-red color, like bark, and for a minute I think I'm bleeding to death.

But then I realize, no, I'm just bleeding for the first time.

I'm afraid to lift myself off the toilet, because I have no idea how fast it comes out and I don't want to make a mess. If I stretch my arms, I can just reach the cabinets below the sink, but when I open them, all I see is a package of cotton balls, a bin of old nail-polish bottles, a sponge, and some bathroom cleaner. I panic and wonder if I've locked the bathroom door and check my cords, but luckily it didn't go through. Finally I decide to take a big wad of toilet paper and fold it back and forth, shoving it into the cradle of my underpants. It feels like everyone will be able to see this giant bulge of tissue and I don't know when we're leaving, so I sneak to the bedroom being used for coats and call Mom.

She's at Aunt Rachel's today. I know the number by heart.

Rach answers. I hear Christmas carols in the background.

"Is anything wrong?" she asks. Her kid is at her ex's today, so it's just the two of them.

"No, but could I just talk to my mom for a second?"

Mom is laughing as she picks up the phone. "Are you having fun?"

"Well, sort of," I say.

"Why are you whispering?" Her voice gets more serious.

"Because they don't know I'm calling you."

"Emma, did something happen? Where's your father?"

"He's in the den. No, nothing happened, it's just . . . well, I just got my period."

"Oh," she says, relieved. "Oh!" she says again, realizing this time what I said. "Well! That's . . . good. Do you have anything there?"

"No, and neither does Aunt Betty, so I just shoved a bunch of toilet paper in my pants." I swear I think I hear her giggle. "Mom!"

"No, what, that's a good idea. That'll be okay until you get home. Don't worry, I've got stuff there. It's just a few hours. Really! If you don't want to wait, why don't you go ask your father to take you to the store—"

"NO way," I say. "DON'T tell him!"

"Okay, okay, I won't. Just don't worry, you'll be home soon. Why don't you go play a board game with Jack or something? I'll see you in a little bit, okay?"

I hang up the phone. I thought that when it happened it would be more like a Judy Blume book, with Mom making me a special period cake or pulling out a kit she'd prepared with every supply inside I could think of. In my version, no one giggles or watches football or smokes brown cigarettes, or asks where my father is. He's in the same house, downstairs reading the paper, while Mom and I decide on what frosting to use and bake us a secret girls-only celebration.

* * * * *

The first day with my new skis the bus heads to Mount Holly. Mike and Stephanie are still sitting together, but they've stopped blowing on windows and writing hearts and promises in the condensation. They've also stopped sharing juice boxes and whispering in each other's ears. Mostly, Stephanie leans over the back of her seat to talk to Brian Van Eden again. Mike cranks his tape player, his headphones secured tightly.

Maybe they won't make it to St. Paul's after all.

I decide to be brave and try a midlevel run by myself on the back end of Mount Holly. This seems to be where Mike Cleveland spends most of his time. The slope is much icier than it seemed from the top, and within a minute after pushing off, I am heading straight for a fence that runs alongside the hill, its wooden planks worn and weathered into a shade of gray. I remember Katrina's advice and lean to fall toward one side, but it's too late. My knees hit the fence full force and there's a loud cracking sound, like a great bolt of thunder next to my ear.

I am lying in the snow, still and dazed and convinced there's a pool of blood around my shattered, useless legs. I push myself up into a sitting position to assess the damage. One ski rests a few feet from me in the snow. I don't see any blood and though my knees sting, I can bend them. I bring the ski that's still attached closer to me and see I've cracked the tip. It dangles like a loose tooth.

Somewhere on the summit, Mike Cleveland is preparing to launch himself down the mountain, possibly right in my direction. But things have changed now. Things are broken, and I pop my damaged ski off my boot, grab what is intact, and walk down the hill on my own.

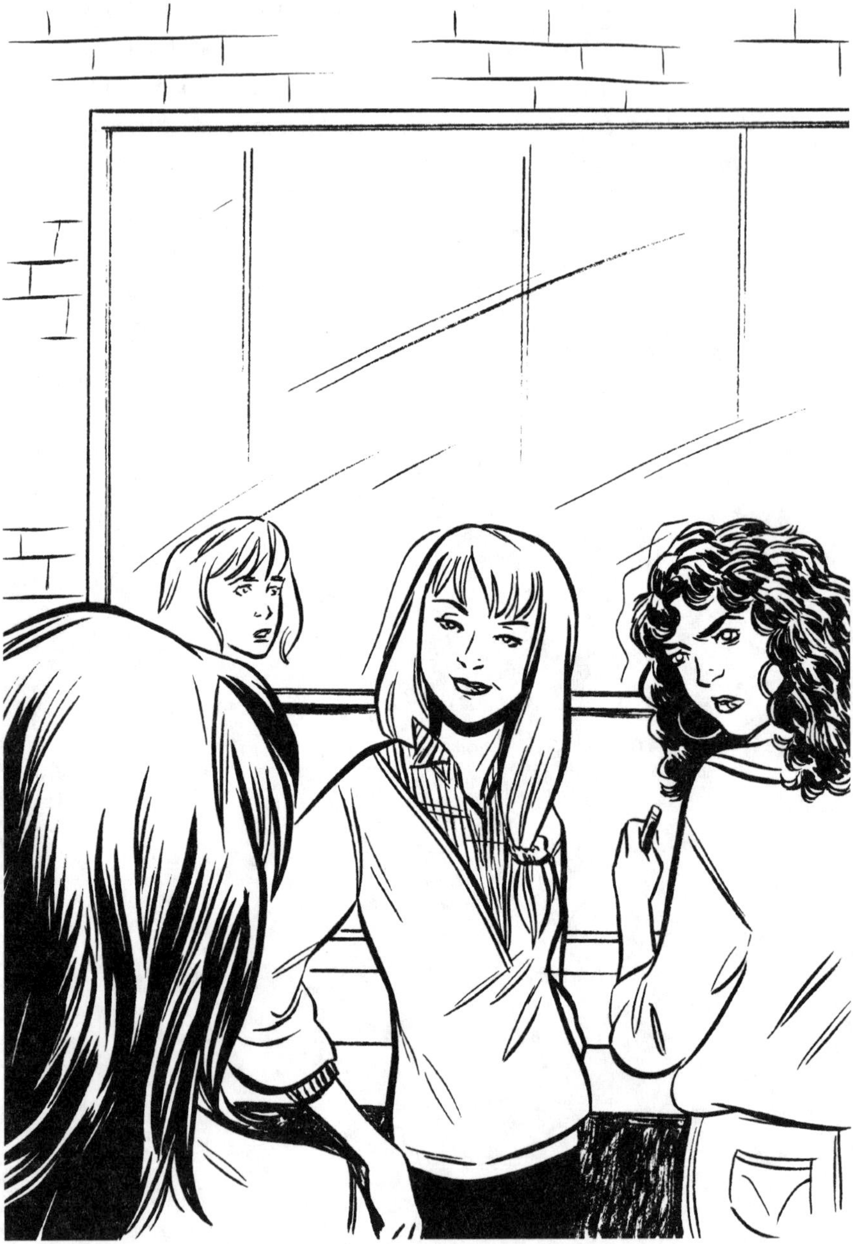

Chapter 5

What People Are Saying About You

The conversation I'm not supposed to hear begins like this:

"Katrina Krause gave Chris Bailey a bj behind Perry's drugstore in the Hill."

It's Stephanie DeMarco's voice. I am in the second-floor girls' bathroom, last stall on the left. I pull my feet up off the ground in case they check, holding my ankles, my breath, hovering and waiting.

"No way!" It's one of her ladies-in-waiting, possibly Megan Hunter. "How do you know?"

"Brian told me," Stephanie says. The Van Eden–DeMarco union was reinstated a few months ago. "Todd told him, and he found out from Chris himself."

"When?"

"Last weekend, during the homecoming game up at the high school."

Bitch. Lying bitch.

"Why did they go to the *high school* homecoming game?"

"Chris's brother plays varsity."

True.

"They left at halftime and walked up to the Hill."

False. We all left during halftime—me, Katrina, and Chris—and the only thing anyone got in the Hill was some blue moon ice cream from Over the Rainbow. Chris and Katrina have been going together since last March at the Winter White War Memorial dance. Anything that lasts longer than six months is considered common-law marriage at Brownell. I'm their official third wheel. Two weeks ago, Katrina told me she finally let him go up her shirt, but over the bra only.

I rehearse my confrontation and flush the toilet as a warning. When Megan sees me, she suddenly becomes fascinated with her Jack Rogers sandals but Stephanie looks me directly in the eye. I break our stare first.

"Hey, Emma," Stephanie says, acknowledging her victory by turning back to the mirror to finish glossing her lips. She takes her time with the wand, tracing the outline of her mouth in gooey raspberry.

"Hi, Stephanie." The sheen of her lips hypnotizes me. I can't remember what comes next. "Listen . . . I . . . you guys should know—"

"I love your top," she says. It's my favorite shirt, a white Esprit blouse with red polka dots. "Could I borrow it sometime?"

"I don't think we're the same size." It slips out before I can stop it.

"Of course we are." Stephanie DeMarco and her perky-but-not-too-big breasts have just declared that we are the same size. I pray for a hidden microphone in the bathroom broadcasting this statement through the PA system.

"Don't forget, the choir is holding their annual bake sale all week in the main lobby, before and after school and during lunch. Also this week, sign up for talent show tryouts in Mr. Koval's office. And finally, Stephanie DeMarco has declared that she and Emma Harris are the same size—please make a note of it."

Focus. Focus. "Listen, Stephanie—"

"Emma, do you have a Halloween costume yet?"

"No, not really."

"None of us knows what we're going to dress up as. We're going to Eastland Mall on Saturday to get ideas. Why don't you come with us?"

"Uh . . ." Megan tries to interject, looking horrified, as if Stephanie has just picked up a cockroach and is petting it like a cat.

Stephanie holds up one hand toward Megan and continues.

"Where do you live? My mom's driving. We'll come by and pick you up around noon."

I think about the apartment that we moved into after the divorce, the bright-green shag carpeting we're not allowed to replace, and the peeling wallpaper in my room that's half the size of my old one. I think about my address on the outskirts of town, barely within the city limits. I think about old Mrs. Tatterton, who lives in the apartment below us, and the smell of the cabbage she boils for soup almost every day, how it seeps through the vents and lingers in our air.

"I'll just meet you there. At the food court?"

"Okay. Suit yourself. Write down your number just in

case," Stephanie says, offering me her red notebook. "On the back, here," she says, pointing to an open spot near a doodle of her initials and Brian Van Eden's, inside a heart.

"Bring your shirt," she adds. "I'll make you a trade. I have just the thing."

And then they're both gone, as if I had imagined all of it. My silence has been bought—for now.

★ ★ ★ ★ ★

"What are you doing Saturday?" Katrina asks me as we're walking home from school a few hours later. Usually we walk to her house and then Mom picks me up when she gets off work. Most of the Grosse Pointe mothers are home during the day, but mine now reports to an office Monday through Friday to assist a stockbroker with charts and files and letters and flights and coffee.

The leaves are already changing and beginning to fall, just a few here and there, crisp and parched. I kick at them with my feet, scuffing the tips of my shoes.

"Nothing really."

"You want to go to the movies? We could watch my *Dirty Dancing* video again. 'Nobody puts Baby in the corner!'" Katrina quotes. She's completely obsessed with Patrick Swayze.

"Um, actually, you know what? I can't. I have this thing."

"What thing? With your mom?"

"Not exactly. It's no big deal," I say.

Katrina stops walking to pick up one of the leaves, yellow as a raincoat, twirling it by the stem. "With your dad?"

"No, no. I just might go with Stephanie and some other girls to look for Halloween costumes."

"Stephanie who? DeMarco?" She laughs. "Right."

"No, really." I start walking again. Katrina lingers behind me for a second, then follows. "It's not a big deal."

"Yeah, it's not."

"Yeah."

We walk in silence.

"So when did you talk to her?"

"Yesterday, in the bathroom."

"Oh."

"I could ask if you could come too—"

"You know what, I forgot, I can't do anything this Saturday. I'm supposed to help my mom get ready for our garage sale. It's in a week." We reach her corner. I look over at my old yard. Someone has left a Big Wheel out in front. The house must have been sold to a younger family. Lilacs have replaced Mom's daffodils. The trim has been repainted sage green.

"You're still coming over next weekend to help with the garage sale, right?"

"Of course," I tell her.

We go inside and find the snack of sliced peaches and graham crackers Mrs. Krause made for us and take it down to the basement den. We settle in for the last twenty minutes of *General Hospital*. When Luke tells Laura he's still in love with her and the credits roll, Katrina passes me the plate and says, "Here. You can have the last cracker," and begins to search through her pile of tapes for Madonna so we can practice our latest dance routine a few times before Mom pulls up in the driveway and honks the horn.

* * * * *

On Saturday morning, I make sure I'm awake, showered, and dressed by nine. I sit with Jack in the living room watching cartoons and picking at a bowl of Rice Krispies without milk.

"Why are you all dressed up?" he snorts, inhaling his third bowl while Pee Wee greets Cowboy Curtis on the television.

"I'm not! Shut up!"

I go back upstairs and change my outfit three more times before Mom yells that it's time to go.

* * * * *

"Why isn't Katrina with you?" Mom asks, pulling into the mall parking lot.

"She had to baby-sit," I lie.

"For who, the Coopers?"

"Uh, yeah."

"Emma, I hope you didn't turn down that job. You should take any baby-sitting job you get offered. Things are different now with allowances."

"I know that things are different, Mother. I'm not stupid." It comes out harder than I wanted it to. "I didn't turn down the job. The Coopers called Katrina first." Lying has become easier since the divorce. I flip up the collar on my pink Polo shirt. It's the only one I own, but Stephanie DeMarco and her girls don't know that. Yet.

"When am I picking you up?" she says for the fifth time, pulling our car in front of JCPenney because it is closest to the food court.

"I don't know, Mom. Four? I'll call you." I jump out and slam the door too hard.

My eyes scan the food court. I don't know what I'm doing. Stephanie DeMarco has said a total of six words to me before this week, and now I'm expecting her to show up and take me shopping with her? I begged Mom to wash the shirt I wore last Tuesday even though we don't usually do laundry until Sunday. It's stuffed into a plastic Kroger shopping bag inside my Le Sportsac purse. Mom would kill me if she found out I was loaning this shirt to a girl she'd never even met.

I wonder if Stephanie will think our fabric softener smells weird.

I scan the food court. Burgers, french fries, ice-cream cones, hot pretzels with mustard or cheese, tacos, but no Stephanie DeMarco. She's not going to show. They're hiding behind the Hot Dog on a Stick counter, taking pictures of me waiting, alone.

The giggle comes through the food court like a wave working its way toward the shore. It's Stephanie's, light and tidy and polite, and her girls try their best to mimic it.

"Fuck." Stephanie tosses it out as soon as she's close enough to me to see if I flinch. It rolls off her tongue, drips fluent and flawless, like a diamond.

"What?" I say.

"We went to Foot Locker to find you instead of the food court. I have no idea why I kept thinking Foot Locker. Isn't that funny?"

Her girls laugh. Megan Hunter. Kelly Davis. Heather McCain. I laugh too. "Fuck," I say. "That's hilarious."

* * * * *

The shopping bags are nestled at our feet. Stephanie is going as Cleopatra. Megan is Robin Hood. Kelly is a cat. Heather is a bunny.

They picked out a monkey costume for me. "It's so cute," they all said. "It's so perfect."

We're back at the food court again. Stephanie and I have made our exchange, my favorite shirt for three plastic bracelets she usually wears on her left wrist.

It's one of her signature styles.

Mom is meeting me at the JCPenney entrance in fifteen minutes. In front of us, there's a tray with chili and cheese fries. We've each had two.

I kept count.

We sip on Diet Cokes.

"So, Emma," Stephanie says. "That Katrina girl. She's going with Chris Bailey, huh?"

"Yeah," I say, sucking on my straw, remembering my purpose. "The thing is . . . they—"

"That's so weird," Heather says. "I thought he liked you."

"What?" I say. "Oh no. We just hang out sometimes. All three of us." I try to look at my watch without being obvious.

"That's not what I heard," Stephanie says, twirling a piece of her caramel hair.

"You know, I think you guys might have the wrong idea about Katrina." I stand up and collect my bags.

"Oh no," Stephanie says. "We don't. Really. Do you have to go?"

"Yeah," I say, throwing my plastic cup in the trash.

"I'll call you later," Stephanie says, waving with her tan, polished hand.

I walk out to meet Mom half drunk.

"How was your afternoon?" she asks, still in her house-cleaning clothes.

"Stephanie DeMarco is going to call me later," I tell her like a robot.

"Is that a good thing?"

★ ★ ★ ★ ★

On Monday, I make Mom drop me off at school late by faking a stomachache in the morning. I spend the lunch hour making up my first-period test. After school, Katrina has band practice, so I slip out without incident. Instead, I meet Stephanie and Megan and Kelly and Heather at Jacobson's in the Village to try on plaid skirts.

On Tuesday, I run into Katrina between second and third period, in the bathroom, first floor.

"Where have you been?" I ask her. "I've been looking for you everywhere."

Katrina stares at me. "I think you should know what people are saying."

"About what?"

"About you."

"Oh really? What's that?"

"They're just using you, you know."

I pull my comb out of my purse and run it through my hair three times before I answer. "Jealous much?"

I say it just like Stephanie DeMarco.

Katrina backs out of the bathroom, shaking her head.

★ ★ ★ ★ ★

On Friday, in between sixth and seventh periods, Stephanie and I dash to the girls' bathroom for a touch-up. As we walk in, someone bumps into me. It's an accident, a crowded doorway and too many girls, but when I look up, Katrina is staring at me.

"Sorry," she mumbles and disappears.

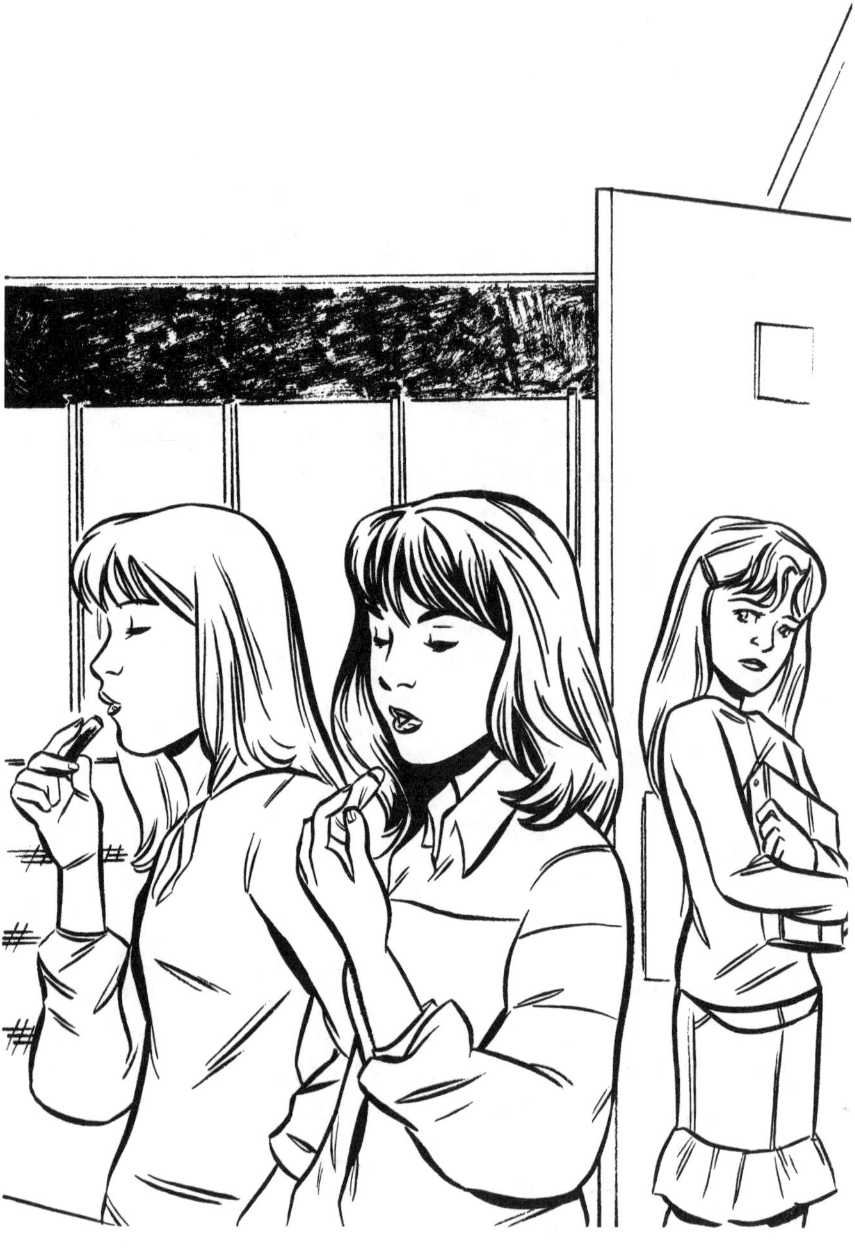

I pause in the doorway.
Stephanie watches me in the mirror.
"If you still want to be friends with her—"
"I don't," I say, waiting for her to pass over her lip gloss,
reaching toward her reflection.

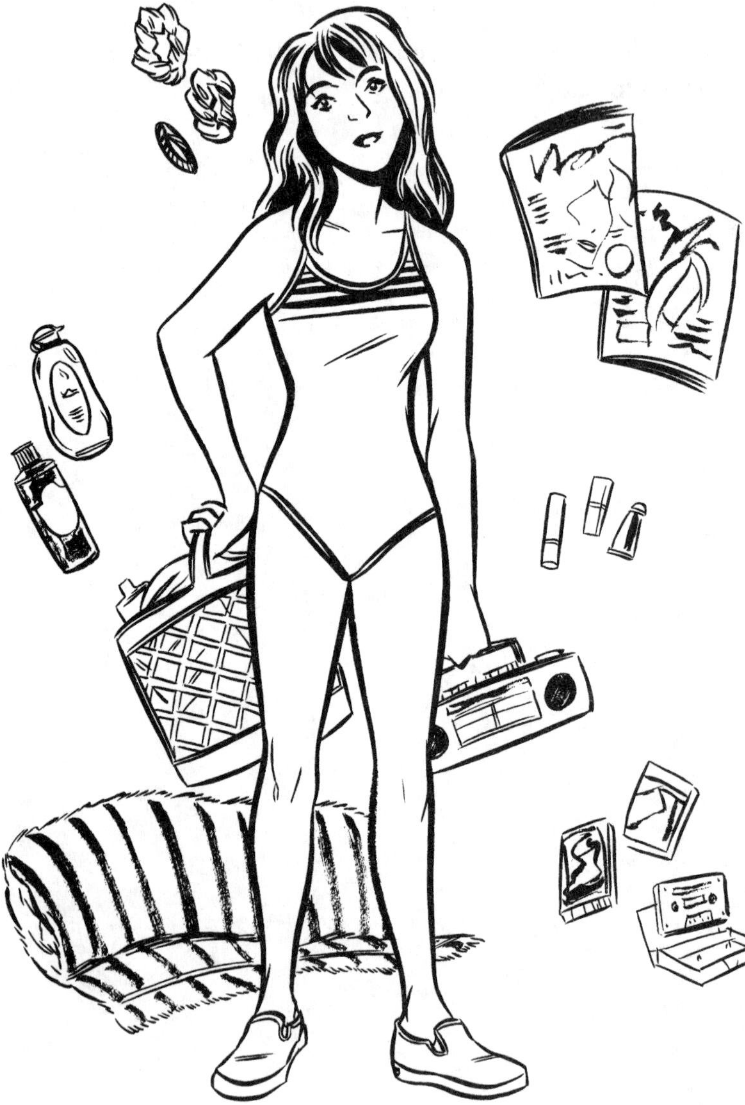

6

Exile from Farms Pier

"Light me a cigarette, will you?"

Stephanie DeMarco, the reigning queen in the Court of Cool, commands me from her bobbing black inner tube within reaching distance of the main pier.

"Yeah, get one for me too," adds the king of the court, Brian Van Eden, as he swims in the waters of Lake St. Clair beside Stephanie's throne. I am a minion in this kingdom, and we minions serve regardless of gender.

It's another test. There have been several in the past nine months. I've never even had a cigarette in my mouth, let alone smoked one, and she knows this.

I crouch down to shield what I am doing, the seat of my swimsuit pilled from wearing it since last season. Shaking out two Marlboro Lights, I hold them in one hand and with the other flick her clear plastic red lighter near the tobacco end of the sticks. It's like setting off fireworks on the Fourth of July, except I can't dash away and there's no explosion. I'm left holding dynamite poppers that turn out to be duds.

I walk to the edge of the pier, holding one cig in each hand between my index and middle fingers, imitating the shiny, slick magazine ads.

"Thanks," Stephanie says, reaching for both smokes.

Test passed.

I am confident, calm.

I am cool.

* * * * *

This summer, Stephanie DeMarco's ladies-in-waiting include Megan, Kelly, Heather, and me. I was certain the trips to the mall and the clothes trading with the royal entourage would fade away as soon as school ended. But on the last day of classes, Stephanie summoned me to her house for their traditional shaving-crème-and-water-balloon fight.

"I hope you don't mind if your clothes get dirty," she said.

I think I took more hits than anyone, especially when the Boys came over and joined, but I didn't complain or cry once. Later, when Mom insisted I tell her who was responsible for my drenched clothes, I told her I was an innocent bystander who had just been caught in the storm.

After this initiation, I learned the daily routines quickly. We begin at eleven A.M. with a car pool coordinated the night before, burdening our mothers with pickups and drop-offs depending on their hair appointments and tennis times. This season, the cool beach bag is a plastic basket style, and we all carry different colors stuffed with freshly washed striped towels from Jacobson's department store. We pack them fresh from the dryer when they are still warm and almost too thick to roll. The lotion loaded with SPF that our mothers force us to bring is replaced with the baby oil stolen from underneath their bathroom cabinets. I also carry the latest issues of *YM* and *Sassy*, and a tube of L'Oréal frosty pink lipstick stolen three months ago from Schettler's during another test. All this, plus two hair scrunchys and a few tapes to put in Stephanie's bubble-gum pink jam box with the mint-green buttons. I bring Guns n' Roses and Depeche Mode but leave Belinda Carlisle at home because I know the Boys will make fun of me.

The Boys are Brian Van Eden, Tim Osborne, Todd Anderson, and Mike Cleveland. They come to the pier every day too, though usually an hour later than we do because they are casual. They are always casual. The Boys do not bring bags or supplies. They come armed only with attitude, some with packs of cigarettes, Marlboro reds of course. Our towels are shared or wound tight with the ends dipped in water to snap at our behinds. Sometimes the Boys also bring a homemade tape of their garage band, and when they pop it into the jam box, Stephanie and Megan sing along to show their support.

I want to sing along too but I can barely hear the words.

"You are . . . fire . . . I have . . . desire . . . Nightstalker . . . Firewalker . . . we are . . . Nightstalker . . . on fire . . ."

I'm not sure, so I just pretend, mouthing nothing into the air, and flip the pages of my magazine, trying to find out "How to Turn That Crush into a Boyfriend" because he is standing right in front of me. Once again, it's Mike Cleveland, with Stephanie's blessing of course. Earlier in the week, he loaned me his Rolling Stones tape when I pretended to like them too. Twice he's chosen my towel to share. I have added these facts and details to my blue-and-green-plaid diary. I'm on page twenty-seven of the Mike Cleveland regime and it's only been a week.

We tend to stay planted on the docks, away from the pool-side parents who could narc to our own about the cigarettes and noise. But the Boys like to show off their cannonballs, back flips, front flips, and handsprings. If they are too lazy to go to the boards, their moves are dangerously executed off the main pier that clearly says "No Diving." The pier lifeguards look the other way because usually the person keeping watch is an older sibling of someone in our group. These high school juniors and seniors once governed the Court of Cool themselves and know the importance of getting away with certain things.

Today the Boys have brought a backpack stuffed with a few suntan lotion bottles. The cream has been washed out of the brown plastic, replaced with whatever liquor one parent had the most of so they wouldn't notice a skim off the top.

"Here," Mike Cleveland says, passing the bottle to me. I make a mental note to record this moment in my diary later and take a baby sip, the juice fruity and burning. I can taste Megan's Dr Pepper Bonne Bell Lip Smackers on the neck of the bottle.

Then we turn up "Sweet Child O' Mine" on the ghetto blaster and dance on our towels like Axl Rose, swinging our legs from side to side without moving the tops of our bodies. Our singing is loud and off-key, annoying the seagulls and the men washing the boats docked nearby. The Boys play air guitar and the Girls keep their sunglasses on and try to look cool, and smoke.

We imagine this is what it is like to be drunk.

* * * * *

On Friday, Stephanie DeMarco's parents are going up north for the Mackinaw boat races, leaving her seventeen-year-old sister, Becky, in charge. Word of the party has been spreading for weeks. Becky promised Stephanie she could have both the Girls and the Boys over, throwing in a bribe of Boone's Farm and Sun Country wine.

We have all crafted and rehearsed our sleep-over stories.

I have been told more than once to stop asking, "What if we get caught?"

* * * * *

When the one o'clock adult-swim whistle blows, it's time for the daily trip to the concession stand for licorice ropes and ice-cream sandwiches. This requires tied towels around our waists, but slung low, just below our hips. This usually means the bottom of the towel drags on the sidewalk, but this is the sacrifice you make to do the right thing.

We are sent in pairs for food.

"Emma, why don't you go with Mike?" Stephanie declares her nomination and the setup is clear. Her hair is sprayed generously with Sun-In and tied loosely at the nape of her neck, her face hidden behind the newest style of Ray Ban sunglasses.

As the group passes crumpled dollar bills into our hands, I try to remember what the Girls have shared. Don't fidget. Arch your back. Laugh at his jokes, but act like you can't stand him.

The Boys shove Mike and say something in his ear that makes him laugh before we walk away. I try to catch Stephanie's eye but her head is buried in the magazine I left open on my towel.

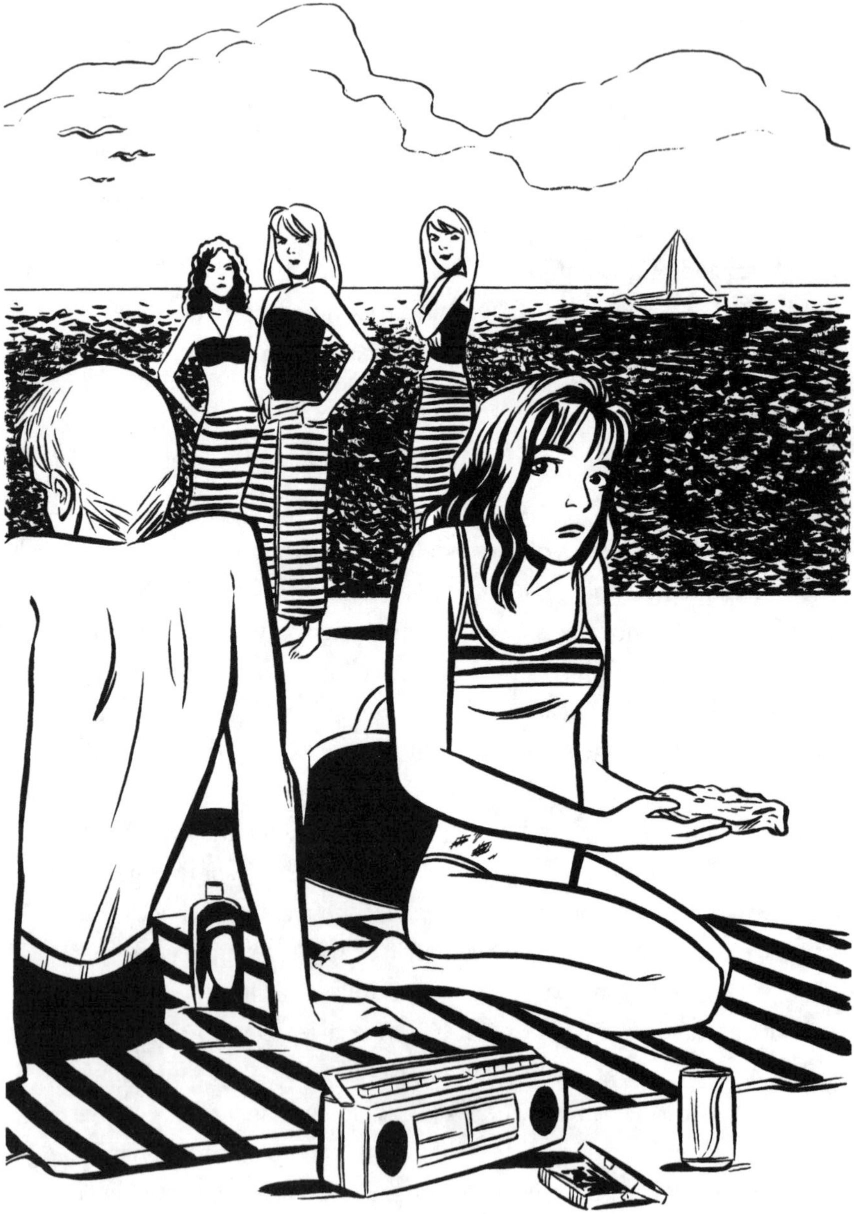

Mike and I walk off the pier and past the guardhouse while I fidget with the money in my hands.

"You wanna go by the tennis courts for a while?" he says. I nod, following him to the courts on the opposite side of the park near the lake.

There's only one lesson going on and we sit on top of a nearby picnic table. Eyes downcast, I stare at old, dried-up bird droppings and a cluster of ants swarming a leftover apple chunk.

Mike is sitting so close to me I can feel his tangy alcohol breath on my neck.

"Emma," he says, just once, and when I look up, his tongue hits my mouth before his lips do. I let him swirl around for a minute, trying to figure out if I should mirror what he's doing or just stay open like a fish. Then his hand goes up toward the top of my suit.

"I think we should get the food. Everyone's waiting."

"What's wrong?"

"Nothing. I'm just hungry and they're waiting."

Mike stands up from the table, brushing away the small twigs stuck to the back of his wet shorts. "Why do you worry so much about everything?"

"I don't," I say. "Really!" But he is already three feet ahead of me.

We wait in line in silence, my hands crossed over my well-blossomed chest, my eyes pretending to concentrate on the food board.

"What should we get?" he asks, his voice hard, defeated.

I shrug my shoulders, unable to talk, so I point to the words: pizza, nachos, Lemonheads. He looks at me for a moment, and shakes his head slowly, giving our order to a short, fat woman with a hair net over her ponytail. We are walking back, and I struggle to balance the food on top of the pop.

When we reach the towels and distribute the goods, I keep one of the square slices of pepperoni pizza for myself. Just before I take my first bite, I notice that the Boys are the only ones eating. The Girls are positioned on the towels, faceup, painted fingernails resting lightly on hipbones, pretending not to see me or the greasy piece of cheese and thick, undercooked dough I am about to sink my ceramic-braced teeth into.

I pause, then pass the piece to Mike and say, "This is yours," and try to lie down like the rest of them. But the grease leaves stains on my suit, fingerprints. There are dark, soiled marks on either side of my hips. I am blemished, and there is evidence.

"Are you done with that tape I loaned you yet?" Mike asks, mouth full of cheese and dough.

I nod and think about how many pages this afternoon will take up in my diary, and just what my actions have cost me.

* * * * *

I get the phone call on Friday morning.

"Hey, Emma, it's Megan."

Stephanie has delegated the task to one of her princesses.

"Hey, Megan."

The verdict is short, brief, direct.

"Listen, I need to talk to you about Becky DeMarco's party. Turns out she won't let Stephanie bring over all of her friends, just a handful. It's really not going to be a big deal anyway. You understand, right?"

"Of course," I say. I swallow hard. I will not break. "So are we going to the pool today?"

"I'm not sure," Megan lies. "Call you later?"

"Okay," I say to the dial tone.

* * * * *

By 11:14 A.M. Mom notices I'm not perched by the front door.

"Are we late? Is it my turn to drive?"

"No," I say. "Actually, we're all getting our own rides today. I forgot to ask. Can you drop me?"

"I have to go up to the Hill anyway," Mom says. "Farms Pier is on the way."

"Oh, we're meeting at the city pool today."

"Really? Okay. Get your things."

* * * * *

The city of Grosse Pointe pool does not have a high dive. There's no concession stand or dock to lie out on. The pool is half the size of the Farms Pier pool. But it's also outside the reign of Stephanie DeMarco.

I walk the deck alone, my hand shielding my eyes as I pretend to look for someone.

"Hey, Emma!"

Lucy Marcus sits up on her towel. We shared gym together this year and she kept the same slow pace I did during warm-up laps. She's also the only other girl I know who's been wearing a bra since sixth grade. We traded this secret during track season as our gym teacher Sarge barked out, "Pick it up, Marcus and Harris!," secretly giving him the finger behind his back every time we finished a lap.

"Hey, Lucy!"

"What are you doing here? I haven't seen you at this pool all summer."

"I'm supposed to meet a friend of mine . . . but I don't see her."

"Well, you can sit with us while you wait if you want," she says. "You know Jennifer and Christina, right?" The girls on either side of her wave.

I move to take my spot at the end of their row.

"Wait," Lucy says. "I'll scoot over," separating the group to put me in the middle.

"So what time is your friend supposed to be here?" she asks, passing me an open bag of tortilla chips.

"I forget," I tell her, placing one in my mouth, and nibble my way into a democracy.

7

The Beginning of
Billy Crandall

Billy Crandall crashes into me freshman year near the thirty-yard line on the football field of our high school. He manages to catch the ball and my legs at the same time and we go down together in a heap.

"Sorry about that," he says as we untangle. His face is inches from mine. There are three freckles under his right eye. He smells like a Christmas tree.

"That's okay," I say, laughing under the weight of his body. "I didn't think anyone would find me out here." I had planted myself off to the edge, near the running track that circles the field, thinking that it was the safest place to hide.

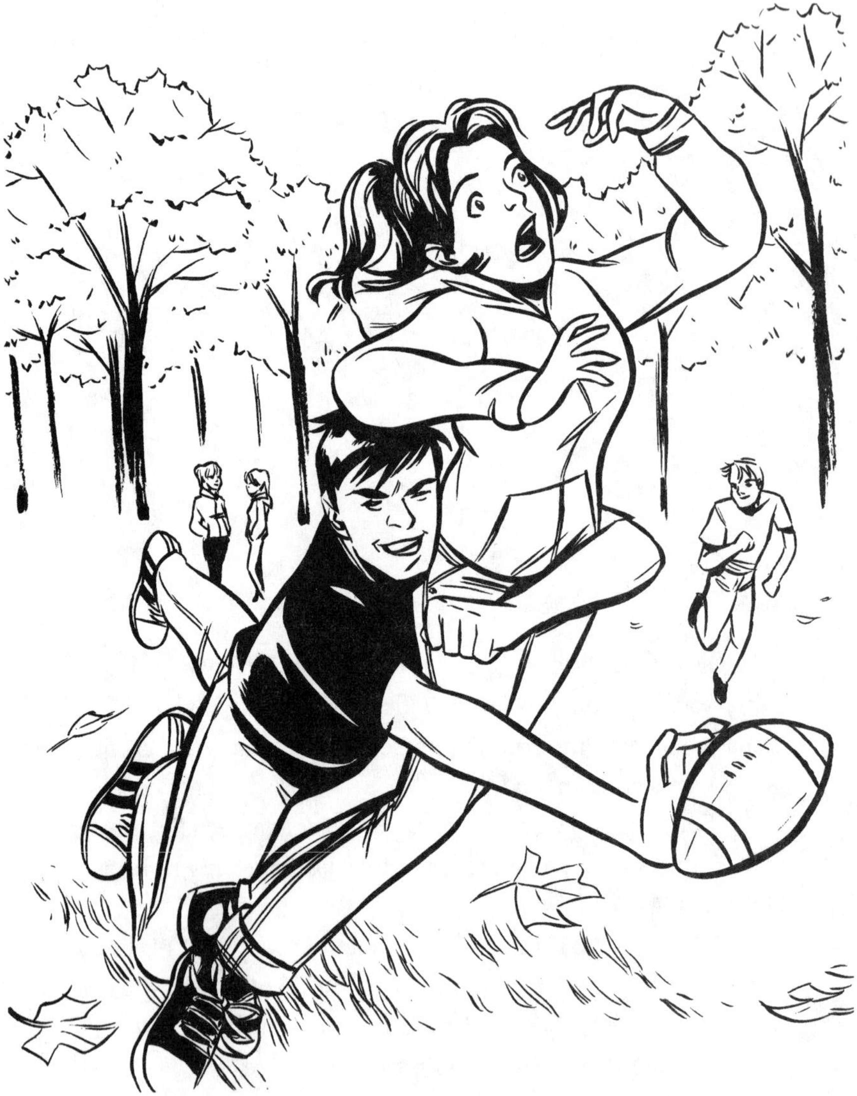

Billy, on the other hand, had started at the center position, in the heart of all the action.

"Guess you were wrong," he says before rejoining the huddle.

My new best friend Lucy has been going with Billy's friend Joe for exactly ten days, and that's how we ended up here for this casual game of touch football even though I've never had anything above a C plus in gym class. We wear uniforms of jeans and windbreakers over long-sleeved T-shirts, with our hair tied up in ponytails. Lucy slips closer to me as the boys huddle to discuss the next play.

"What was that all about?" she whispers.

"Nothing. I just got in the way."

Lucy raises her eyebrows. "I'll say."

"Oh shut up."

Billy and Joe and the rest of the boys are making some sort of grunting, chanting sound. The other girls have already taken this opportunity to stray off the field for a quick smoke break, passing just one cigarette between the four of us.

Billy takes his position.

"What's his story anyway?" I ask Lucy.

I'd seen him a few times since I'd started South last fall, mostly just a face passing me in the hallway between classes, or a figure among the cluster of boys in the cafeteria during lunch.

"He went to one of the Catholic middle schools," she tells me. "I think he lives near Alter Road." It's the Grosse Pointe street closest to Detroit and the houses are all small and narrow, some holding two or three families. This area is often referred to as the "Cabbage Patch," usually by the same kids who have elevators in their homes and a BMW waiting for them when they turn sixteen. Mom and Jack and I had finally moved into a small conda a few months ago. It wasn't a house exactly, but it was better than the apartment we'd moved into right after the divorce. I had started bringing friends around again, but I never forgot how close we'd come to Alter Road.

It's Sunday afternoon, the last week of March, but nearly sixty degrees outside. Despite the early spring, clumps of snow coated with dirt linger, refusing to acknowledge the change of season.

We take our positions for the next play. Joe holds the ball and looks for someone to pass to and I notice how close Billy is to me again, fifteen yards, ten, only five.

After two hours of playing, we are muddy messes, a gaggle of boys and girls with an excuse to fall on each other's developing bodies. As the sun falls behind the tree line, we gather up our things from the bleachers and unlock our bikes. Billy waves good-bye to everyone but me.

Then he says, "Hey, Emma?"

"Yeah?" I say, climbing onto my bike.

He's leaning against his ten-speed, a cigarette dangling out of the corner of his mouth. He flips open his lighter, which has some sort of crest on it, and cups his hands around the flame.

"See you later," he says, like he means it.

* * * * *

The next day, Joe passes me a note as we are both walking to the arts building via the second-floor bridge. I unfold the wide-ruled, torn sheet of paper during a lecture about the history of watercolor paintings. Joe's handwriting is shaky and fast, his message brief.

"Do you like Billy?"

I think about Billy Crandall's eyebrows, thick and dark and concerned. I think about the large brown eyes that hide beneath them, round as marbles, wet and shiny and sad. Or how he smiles, a slow, bright grin that lingers in the right corner of his mouth.

I think about his freckles.

I think about Christmas trees.

While sitting through forty more minutes of slides, I draw hearts on my notebook, filling the centers with little B.C.s, only to scratch them out moments later, the dark blue pen making grooves from the pressure.

As soon as the bell rings, I dash two doors down and wait outside the metals class to give Joe my answer.

"I'll have him call you," Joe says, and I remind him that I can't talk on the phone past nine o'clock, just one of the rules Mom instigated after the divorce to prove she was still in control.

* * * * *

The phone call comes that night at 8:14 P.M. The receiver is resting on my lap and I answer it before the end of the first ring.

"Hey," Billy says. I hear him smoking and wonder how he gets away with it at home.

"Hey," I say back. "Where are you?"

"My house. Outside."

"Oh," I say. "Are your parents around?"

"My mom's out with her boyfriend," he tells me.

"My parents are divorced too," I say, wishing I could smoke.

He takes a long drag. "My parents aren't divorced." His exhale sounds like a train coming into the station. "My dad's dead."

I smack my forehead and think about what an asshole I am. "God, I'm sorry—"

"Don't worry about it. Hey, don't you have Mr. Goldsmith for civics?"

"Yeah. Sixth period."

"Thought so, I'm fourth period. He's pretty cool, huh?"

At 8:59 P.M., Mom picks up the other extension and tells me it's time to go. When I hear her hang up, I tell Billy, "It's not my curfew, it's hers."

"Yeah," Billy says and we sit in silence while I imagine an egg timer running out. "So, um, do you want to go together?"

"Okay," I say. Then I take the stairs two at a time to find Mom in the living room watching *L.A. Law* where I beg for special permission to call Lucy for five minutes to tell her the news before bed.

* * * * *

Three weeks later, I wait until 8:51 to call Billy and tell him I've changed my mind.

"Are you breaking up with me?" he asks.

"I guess," I say.

"Why?" We only have minutes to spare.

"I just think we might be better as friends."

He doesn't say anything after the dreaded "just friends" tag so I add, "No, really. I really want to. I mean it."

"All right," he agrees. "So we're friends."

"Yes," I say as I hear the click of the other extension, grateful for the escape. "We are."

* * * * *

During sophomore year on the third Saturday of every month, Billy Crandall takes me to his father's grave. He'll call me around noon and ask, "What are you doing, Harris?"

"Nothing much, Crandall," I'll say, because I like it when we call each other by our last names.

"Pick you up in twenty minutes?" He'll say it like a question, but I never say no.

We call it "going for a drive," but we always end up at the same place. I try to act normal in his car, as if we are just headed for Eastland Mall to catch a movie. Billy drives a dark blue Plymouth Turismo with plush bucket seats. It's his car, so we can smoke in it. He is a die-hard true supporter of Marlboro reds. I have heard the urban legends of smokers coughing up glass, so I stick with Lights, but pass him my box to pack for me. He gives it several hard taps against the base of his palm, flips open the top, rips out the foil, and hands it back to me.

I count out the letters of the alphabet on the top of each filter until I get to Z, which I turn over.

"Lucky cigarette," I explain. "You're supposed to smoke it last." And I do.

Billy and I don't talk about the Z—Zack Thompson, a boy I like who goes to a different high school. We also don't acknowledge that the name on the headstone Billy and I are standing in front of is exactly his own. This particular piece of land around us is reserved for city firefighters, but we do not mention that these men, unlike his father, died on duty.

I don't know many details of his suicide, but I imagine his father's last breath was a cold cloud of smoke that lingered and frosted the windows of the pickup truck, parked in front of the family home, before they were covered with his own blood.

I haven't asked Billy who found him.

The weather always seems to be the same for these trips: a vast almond sky, no sun, but no discernable clouds either, mild with occasional shivers. I usually wait for Billy to speak first.

Today he tells me, "My dad had a pretty good singing voice."

Sometimes we don't say a word. We just stand and wait and watch.

Eventually, he'll take off his leather bomber jacket that smells like woodsy cologne and nicotine and drape it over my shoulders, and I know that means it's time to go.

I don't think he brings anyone else here, but I don't ask.

On the way back, if he tries to say something like "Thank you," I tell him to shut up before he can begin, fiddle with the radio dial, push in the cigarette lighter, and then suggest we get tacos before he takes me home.

★ ★ ★ ★ ★

The parties I go to with Billy Crandall are not Grosse Pointe parties. They are where Detroit edges up to Grosse Pointe, just past the city limits, in houses that have already lived hard, with peeling paint and usually a broken window or two. The Grosse Pointe police can't touch us here. The Detroit cops are usually too busy worrying about abandoned houses being lit on fire or crack deals.

Both Mom and Dad have said, "If I ever catch you in Detroit, you will be grounded for life," but Billy's around our house so much, Mom has stopped asking me where we're going when he picks me up. Most nights I don't have to lie. If I'm with my girlfriends, we just follow the procession of cars back and forth between the same three checkpoints—Schettler's drug store, St. Paul's parking lot, and "the Tree," which is near a cement slope that leads down to Lake St. Clair.

But Billy takes me places I would never otherwise see, places where I'll never come across Stephanie DeMarco and Brian Van Eden. The Detroit parties are usually thrown by one of the guys Billy went to Catholic school with back in junior high. The Catholic schools don't care what your zip code is; they just want tuition bills paid on time. Most of the Catholic-school parents work blue-collar jobs, putting in long hours to keep their kids out of Detroit public schools. These parents do things that keep the city running—lots of cops and EMTs and firefighters, like Billy's dad used to be. After his death, his father's pension couldn't keep up with the tuition. Billy's mom had the good sense to move into her boyfriend's house just inside the Grosse Pointe city limits right before Billy started high school.

"Hey, Emma," a kid named Marshall says and nods to me as we walk up the front-porch steps. He's one of three black kids from my class of over three hundred students. Three, and they are always at the parties Billy Crandall takes me to.

"Hey, Marshall," I say, hugging him as I pass through the door.

They are only at the parties Billy Crandall takes me to.

* * * * *

In the two years since Billy and I first met, dated for what seemed like thirty seconds, and settled into what has been friends ever since, I have never invited him to any birthday parties or holidays at my house.

Ever.

I have reasons.

There's a famous family story that gets told at least once or twice a year, sometimes at Grandma's on Christmas but usually on my birthday, which is in February.

It always starts with, "Emma, I can't believe you're [insert current age here]!"

And then, "I remember right before you turned four, your mom and dad took you to the auto show at Cobo Hall downtown and you said, 'Mom, why are all these people so dark?'"

I don't recall saying this, but everyone else seems to and they laugh every time, like they've never heard the story before. On my last birthday, when apparently it was Uncle Kurt's turn to tell the story, my cousin Leslie, who is twenty and studies sociology at the University of Michigan and doesn't wear makeup or buy leather shoes, said, "You know, I'm offended by the racial undertones of this story."

Everyone stopped laughing and turned to stare at her. Leslie took another sip of her Irish coffee and continued.

"Emma was too young to know what she was saying, but you should have explained to her about different races and cultures instead of encouraging the incident as a basis for humor."

No one moved for several seconds but it seemed like an hour, until Uncle Kurt finally said, "Excuse us," and took Leslie out back while Mom asked who wanted chocolate-chip ice cream with their cake.

★ ★ ★ ★ ★

There's always rap music at these parties and tonight's no different: Tone-Loc, Rob Base, Run-D.M.C. The girls here are mostly from the Catholic schools too. Ever since Lucy stopped seeing Joe, it's been harder for me to get her to come along. But Christina and Jennifer are with me tonight, and Billy never leaves my side. Today falls on my weekend with Dad, but he's out at a black-tie event for the auto show, so I know I can push my curfew by at least thirty minutes and still beat him home.

"Do you want a beer?" Billy yells above "Funky Cold Medina."

"Okay," I yell back, and even though they're charging everyone five bucks for the privilege of a red plastic cup, Billy waves my money away. He leans over to whisper something into the ear of the tall, lanky kid manning the keg, and the boy nods and fills our drinks without any exchange of currency.

"What was that about?" I mouth to Billy as he hands me the cup.

"He owes me a favor," Billy mouths back, sipping the foam off the top. Some of it stays on his upper lip and I reach up to wipe it away with my left hand.

"You want to go outside for a second?" he leans over to scream in my ear. "I kind of want to talk to you about something."

I nod and reach for my purse to make sure I have my cigarettes. We head outside, away from the pulsating beat box and the sticky bodies wall to wall and the eyes of the other girls wondering just what the hell I am doing with the best-looking guy in the room.

* * * * *

Billy Crandall and I are sitting outside on the driveway even though it's January and twenty-three degrees outside. Christina, who has never been a strong drinker, has stumbled outside behind us. She's auditioning next week for this year's

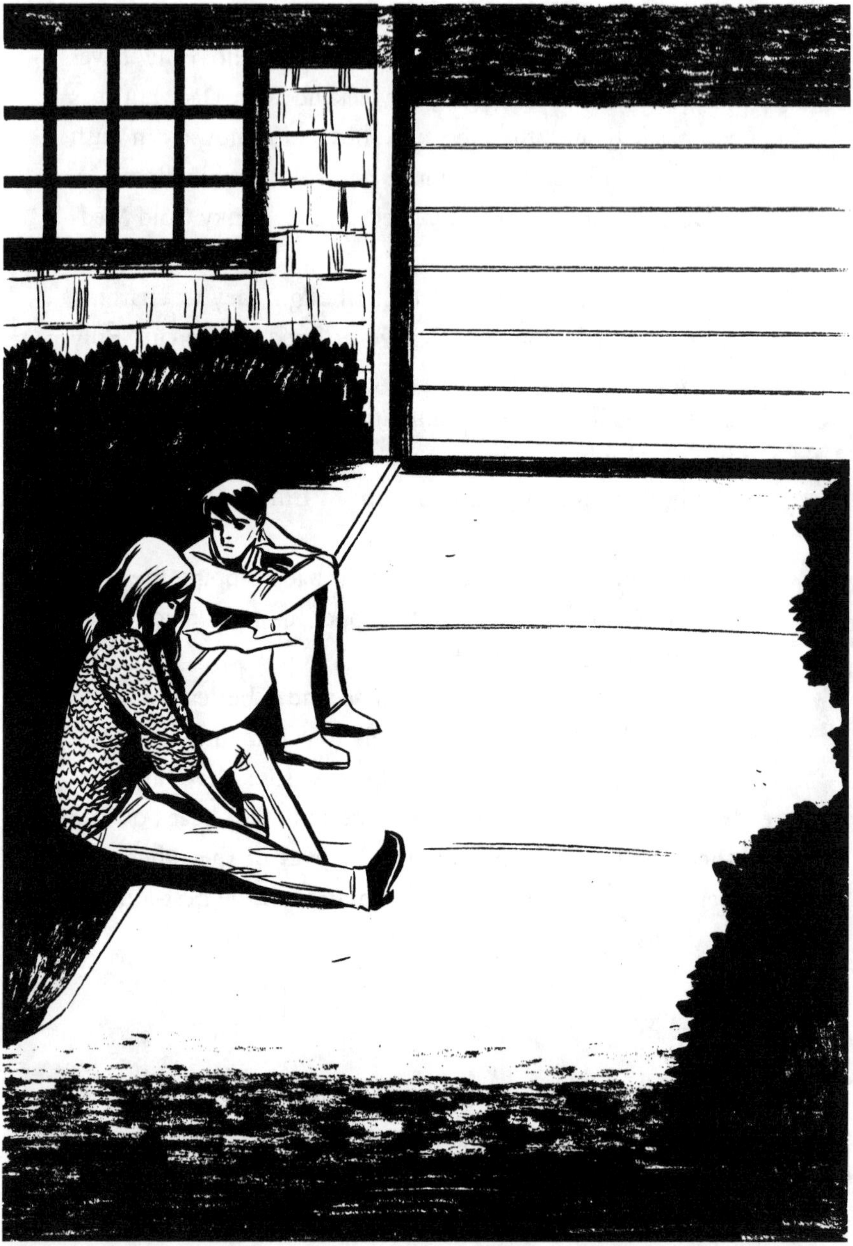

musical, *Anything Goes,* and comes down the driveway doing a little soft-shoe number, almost slipping on the ice. She does not understand that now is not the time for an audition.

After she's tapped three rehearsal numbers, including two false starts, we applaud politely. The encouragement sends her back inside for more fuel, and then we are alone again.

"I need to tell you something," Billy says.

I hold a beer can between my knees, tugging at the silver tab, waiting.

His breath rises to begin a sentence only to exhale, wordless.

It is 11:42 P.M., seventy-eight minutes until curfew. I am thinking about the beer on my breath, reaching for a piece of gum in my pocket, and wondering where Zack Thompson is and if he will call me next week or ignore me again like an itch on his elbow he's just too lazy to scratch.

The late September fog has moved in to embrace us without notice when Billy finally says it. It is not so much a declaration but rather a statement of truth.

The earth is round.

The state stone of Michigan is the Petoskey.

I am in love with you.

* * * * *

I hand Christina's keys to Jennifer and tell them both I'll catch a ride home with Billy that night. We sit outside Dad's house in Billy's car an hour past my curfew. Vintage Eric Clapton plays over and over because the tape is wedged in his stereo and won't come out.

When "Wonderful Tonight" comes on for the fifth time, I finally speak.

"We can't be that way with each other."

"Why not?"

In the distance behind us, I see headlights approaching that might belong to Dad.

"Because I don't want you to end."

Without looking up, I lift the car door handle and slip away from Billy Crandall for now, racing against time and black ice underneath a cold, bruised night.

＊ ＊ ＊ ＊ ＊

"So what's going on with you and Billy?" Lucy asks me in the cafeteria during lunch the following Monday. Christina and Jennifer chew and wait for my answer.

"Nothing. We're just friends." I break a chocolate-chip cookie into bite-size pieces so it doesn't get stuck in my ceramic braces. I get them off in two weeks and four days.

"You sure?" Christina asks, giggling.

"Of course," I say, the dough melting in my mouth, still hot from the oven. "Of course."

Chapter 8

The Lochmoor Moms

Death is unavoidable on the pool deck of the Lochmoor Country Club. The fish flies that swarm by the millions each June do not stand a chance despite the mightiness of their hordes. Biology is working against them. Fish flies live only twenty-four hours and the ones who try to change the rules and fight their destiny are found floating with their defeated brothers and sisters, creating an inch-thick crust on the pool surface. Others are smashed underneath security lights, or perhaps dried up and fallen behind the lounge chairs, leftovers for someone else to sweep away.

This is the battle I fight as a Lochmoor lifeguard. The bugs hit early on during peak swim-team season, late June and July, and we guards are constantly skimming the surface. We use long

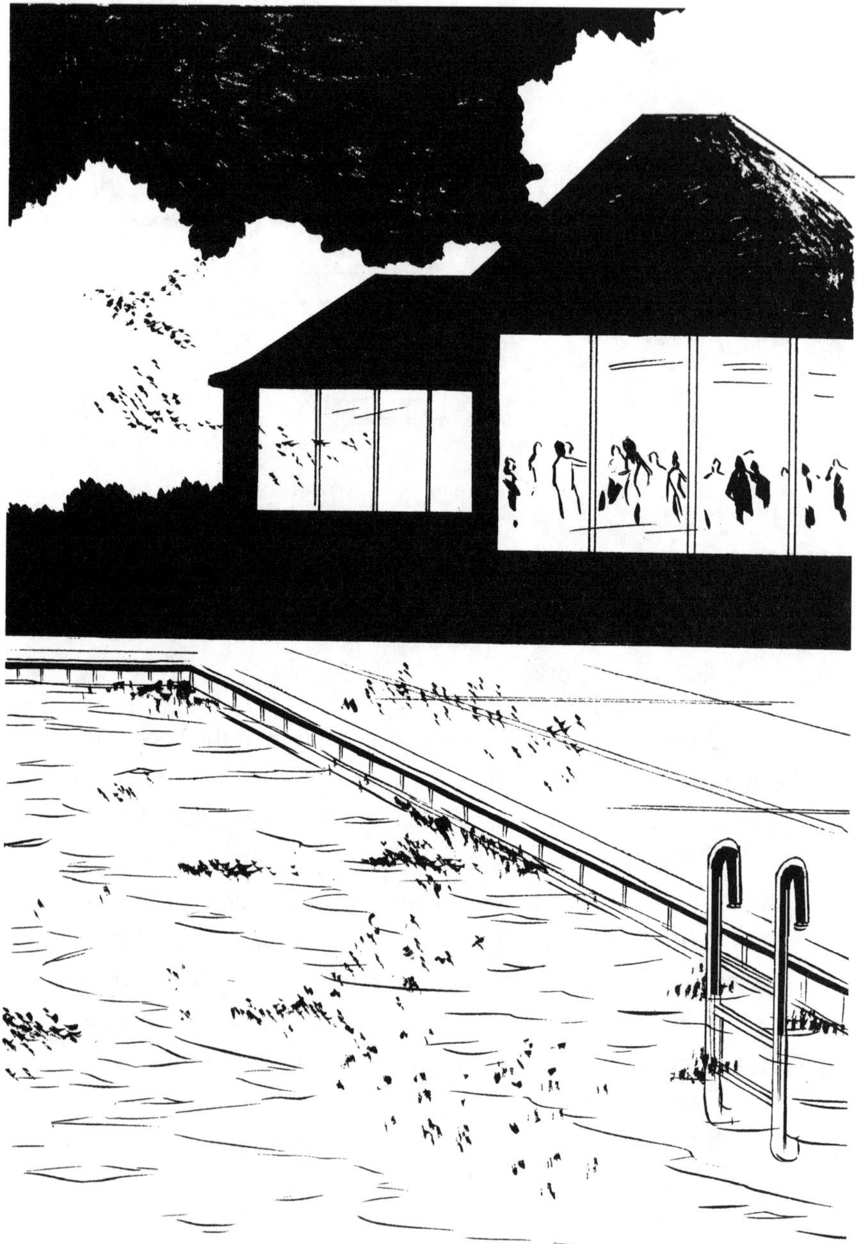

silver poles topped with square baby-blue nets, moving them back and forth as if we are icing cakes. Then the poles are lifted, nets swung above and turned over large gray plastic bins, the bodies dumped with a few strong blows to the edge.

We do this three, sometimes four times a day. We do whatever it takes to make the pool look perfect.

★ ★ ★ ★ ★

The Coopers helped me get the job at Lochmoor.

"We've been members for over ten years," Mr. Cooper told me one night during the pickup. He always handles chauffeur duty because he finishes getting ready first, and that gives Mrs. Cooper an extra fifteen to thirty minutes to finish curling her hair, putting on her nylons, or sometimes even helping the kids get into their pajamas.

"Ten years? Really? Well, I just passed my swimming test and put an application in, so it's probably too soon to hear anything," I tell him while putting my seat belt on, a pile of textbooks and a magazine or two on my lap for after the kids go to bed.

"Nonsense," he says. "It's already mid-April. The pool opens in about six weeks. I know the swim coach. We'll make a call. It'd be great to have someone at the pool the kids already know! They practically live there in the summer."

Mr. Cooper drives a big black luxury sedan because he's an executive for one of the car companies, Ford, I think. It's not the same one my dad works for, but they all seem to know each other. If he picks me up at my dad's house, sometimes Mr. Cooper comes to the door where they make small talk about the auto show or the Grand Prix. But usually I'm at my mom's, and

Mr. Cooper just pulls into my driveway and does two quick honks to let me know he's there.

His car is immaculate but there is a slight smell of smoke that lingers around the leather seats. I think he might sneak one on the way over to pick me up. Sometimes I consider bringing my own secret stash of cigarettes and offering him one, just to see the look on his face.

"How's school?" he asks, because this is how the conversation always goes. "You're at South now, right?" He turns his oldies station down to hear my answer. His front seat is one long leather bench but he's got the divider pulled down between us.

"Yep. I'm a sophomore now," I say.

"A sophomore! Wow! Jeez, I can't believe you're already a sophomore. How long have you been baby-sitting for us now—"

"Three and a half years," I answer, unwrapping a stick of spearmint gum.

There's a lot you can learn about someone in three and a half years. Most of what I know I've learned from Mr. Cooper's walk-in closet after the kids go to sleep. Mr. and Mrs. Cooper have separate closets and each one is the size of my bedroom. His smells like cedar and everything is arranged tidily. He has expensive wood hangers that hold mostly blue suits in perfect form and a separate area for his striped silk ties. His tasseled, polished loafers are all lined up with the toes pointing out and there's a series of drawers built into the wall, one with nothing but jewelry cases of monogrammed cuff links, some in fourteen-carat gold, others in silver.

I've seen his underwear drawer too, and he wears the grown-up kind, white with a thick band around the top.

One time I was standing in the closet smelling his shirts,

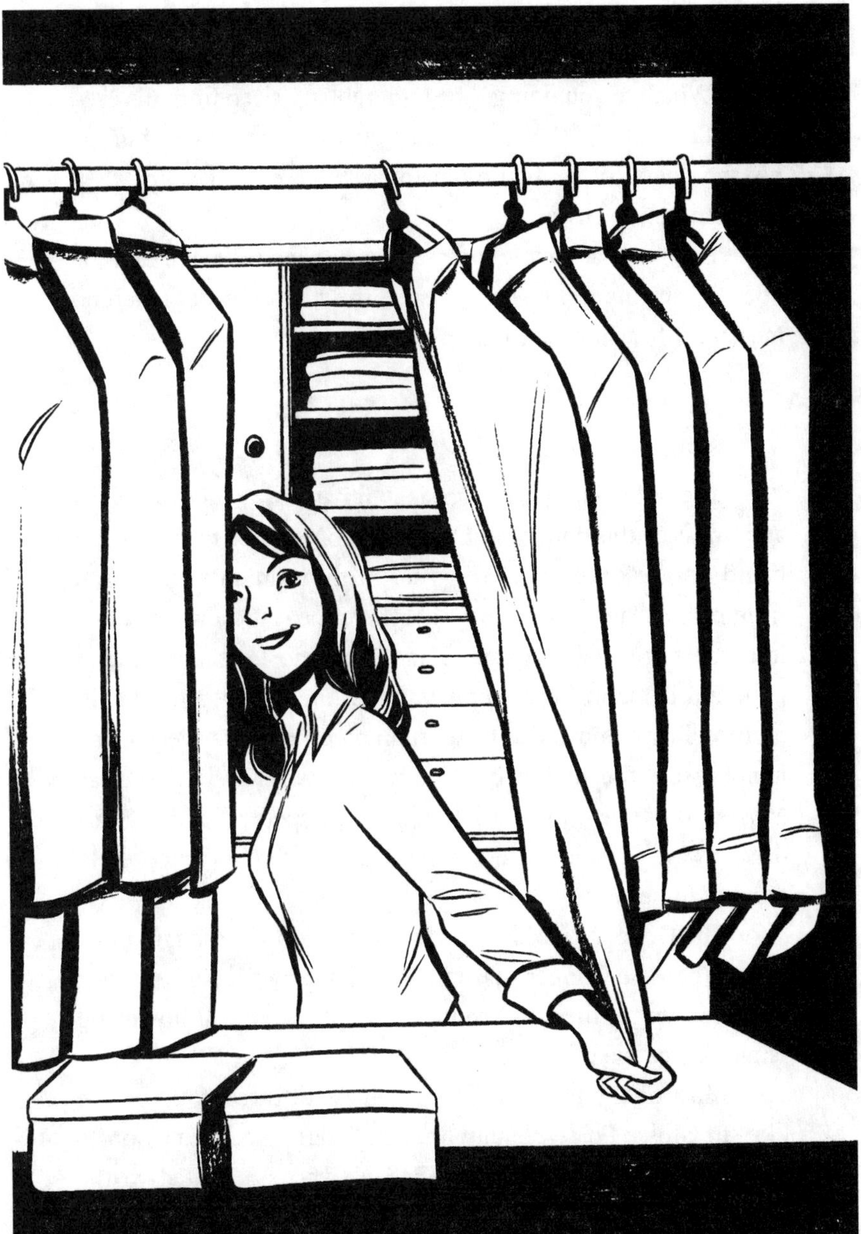

hugging five or six of them to my face, when Jamie, the youngest, wandered in.

"What are you doing?" he said, rubbing sleep from his eyes.

"Looking for the cat," I came up with and guided him by his shoulders to the bathroom for a Dixie cup of water, then returned him to his bed.

This was a couple of months ago and I'm certain he doesn't remember, but now I close the bedroom door behind me, so if I hear it creak, I at least have a warning.

★ ★ ★ ★ ★

The Lochmoor pool is so small it has just two guard chairs and, most of the time, we only use the one closer to the diving board, in the deep end. We go up in thirty-minute shifts, and from here, I have a good view of where the station wagons pull into the tarred parking lot. Sometimes, the Lochmoor moms park and come in for a tennis lesson while we keep their children, yelling commands like no running on the pool deck or no jumping off the diving board until the water below is clear. Most of the time, though, the kids are dropped off and the cars drive away and don't return until after swim practice ends, around dinnertime.

The Cooper kids always stay the latest of all the families.

When the Coopers haven't come back by the time we lock the gates, we let the kids use the office phone to call home and remind someone of where they are.

Most of the families are Catholic with three, four, or five kids. In Grosse Pointe, family lines are intertwined: the Coopers are related by marriage to the Baileys who are related to the Thompsons. The only slow time at the pool is on Sunday mornings when the families of Grosse Pointe congregate at church. Anyone who's anyone attends Star of the Sea's noon mass, followed by a leisurely breakfast at the Pancake House that requires a thirty-minute wait just to be seated.

Sometimes on my break, I eat a grilled turkey-and-cheese sandwich from the snack shack and flip through the club directory, studying the names. Business listings don't always exactly fit with the location of the member's home—like a car wash business and a Lakeshore address—but I've learned not to ask questions around here.

★ ★ ★ ★ ★

"How are you liking Lochmoor?" Mr. Cooper keeps one hand on the steering wheel, driving exactly the speed limit of twenty-five. He shoots me a quick glance and then his eyes are back on the road.

"It's cool," I tell him. "Thanks again for all your help." I fold my hands neatly on my new red skirt I bought with the money from the last two jobs at their house.

"Well, pretty soon, you'll be so busy with all your boyfriends and dates, we'll be lucky if we can get you for even one weekend a month."

"Boyfriends?" I snort. "Hardly."

"Oh, I'm sure there are a million boys after a pretty girl like you."

I mumble something that sounds affirmative and stare out the window at the freshly mowed neighborhood lawns.

"See," Mr. Cooper says as he pulls into his driveway. "That's what I'm talking about!"

★ ★ ★ ★ ★

I was one of two girls in my lifeguarding class of twelve students. The other girl didn't go to my high school and I never learned her name. She was heavier than me, a good twenty to thirty pounds, and her thick wild eyebrows had never known tweezers, the innermost edges reaching for each other, trying to become one.

Our instructor was a former country club swim star, home from college for the summer. On the first day of class, we were ordered into the shallow end of the pool. The boys, Mike Cleveland and Todd Anderson and Tom Mason, plummeted in one by one, knees to chest, their splashes sharp bullets in my eyes. I called them names like "Ass!" and "Shithead!," trying to flip my wet locks away from my face.

The fat girl said nothing because no one was splashing her. Instead, she gnawed at the purple nail polish peeling off her right thumb, her other arm flung across her belly.

I offered her something along the lines of a smile but no words, tugging on the strap of my one-piece bathing suit that was the color of margarine. I was more concerned with how I would endure ten consecutive laps of freestyle in front of these crush-worthy boys. They couldn't possibly be concerned, having been on swim teams since toddler age at their respective country clubs: the Grosse Pointe Yacht Club, the Lochmoor Country Club, the Grosse Pointe Hunt Club, the County Club of Detroit, the Detroit Yacht Club, the Detroit Athletic Club. Of course, the proper way to refer to these establishments is by acronym: GPYC, LCC, GPHC, CCD, DYC, DAC.

I had never been on a swim team. But I was aware of the bottom line: the cool summer job to have in Grosse Pointe was lifeguarding, preferably for one of the area clubs, whichever one you do not belong to.

Choosing one I didn't belong to would not be a problem.

We were administered several tests during the one-week training: the fifty-meter swim, backboard rescues, CPR on a doll we called Annie. The most difficult to pass was treading water for one minute while holding a ten-pound black rubber brick. I was certain I'd fail on my first try, and did. But so did every boy in the class, and the fat girl, so I knew I'd escape ridicule for at least a while longer. The boys lined up at the pool gutter for my second try with the brick.

The fat girl sat off to the side in between the silver bars of the three-step ladder, pretending to concentrate on something underneath the water. Her legs swirled, slow and heavy.

Meanwhile, my last name became the chant of the male tribe.

"Harris! Harris! Harris!"

And suddenly I was the power forward, the running back, the defensive wingman. I was just one of the guys, so I forgot about trying to be a sexy fifteen-year-old and pedaled furiously in twelve feet of overchlorinated water. Sixty seconds became thirty, and thirty became ten, and then ten became zero.

I was still holding the brick, head above water, the boys whooping and hollering, when the fat girl began to cry.

* * * * *

When we walk in the side door to the kitchen, the kids are all at the dinner table. Lindsay is eight, Beth is five, and Jamie is three. Tonight's a Tater Tots and sloppy joe night. Most of Jamie's food is mashed into his fingers or on his shirt, Beth has barely touched hers, and Lindsay has already finished, rinsed her plate, and put it in the dishwasher.

I like it better when the kids have eaten before I arrive so I don't have to coax or make bargains, like three more bites of chicken equals cookie-dough ice cream for dessert. I know the routine because I used to do it myself, how they insist they are too full for another bite of green beans but later on manage to beg for a foil-wrapped Ding Dong before bed. If they're fed before I get there, it's usually Tater Tots or fish sticks with apple-sauce or macaroni. Or if the Coopers are really running behind, there will be a $20 bill on the counter next to a coupon for Domino's.

The last couple of times I've been over, Lindsay has tried to be my little helper of sorts, watching Jamie while I con Beth into bed, or making sure everyone has brushed their teeth and not just run the brushes under the water. Since I don't have any boyfriend to call after they're asleep, I've been letting Lindsay sneak downstairs after the other two are in bed. We watch videos on MTV until we hear the garage door and then she races back to her room to pretend she's been there the entire time.

I hear Mrs. Cooper's heels approaching on the hardwood living-room floor before she clicks into the kitchen. "Oh, hi, Emma! I didn't hear you two come in. Did you kids say hello to Emma?" she asks, fanning her nails dry, a touch-up from her weekly salon manicure.

"Yes, Mom," the chorus of three respond.

"The kids just love having you at the pool." She smiles and turns to her husband. "Honey, would you go get the present from the bedroom? It's on the bed, already wrapped."

Mr. Cooper glances at his watch.

"I swear, I am almost ready." He nods and disappears.

It took only a few weeks of baby-sitting to see why someone like Mr. Cooper would marry her. Mrs. Cooper's hips are a little wide, but otherwise she's in good shape, and when she wears darker pants or skirts you can't even tell. Because she's very tall, she looks even better when she wears something that shows off her legs, like the black wrap dress she has on tonight. Her frosted-blond hair is upswept and sprayed stiff, and on her earlobes she wears long dangling earrings made of tiny diamonds that are probably real. Her magnolia perfume trails her around the kitchen as she wipes up the counter and puts the milk carton away.

I've been through her closet too, but mostly just her cosmetics because I think women have a better sense of whether someone has gone through their things. Her makeup drawer is in the mirrored vanity that sits inside her closet. So far, that drawer is the only thing I've found in the house that's even remotely out of order, and it's a mess. Mrs. Cooper's makeup is the expensive kind you buy at the Hudson's department-store counters. She must get a makeover every season with her numerous plum eye shadows, tubes of thick black mascara, and an eyelash curler I don't know how to work and am afraid to try. She also has glass bottles of perfume lined up along the tabletop, the kind with stoppers that pull out so she can dab her wrists.

She doesn't work, like Mr. Cooper, but I know she has errands and meetings because I've seen them marked on the calendar taped to the inside of the kitchen-pantry door. "Tennis clinic, 3 PM," and "Jamie's playgroup, 2 PM," and "Lindsay–Dentist, Tues 4 PM," and "Art Fest. Committee—War Memorial lunch 12–1 PM."

Mrs. Cooper shows me the list she's left next to the phone: the number of the country club, the last name of the wedding party, the name and number of the next-door neighbor, 911 of course, poison control, and the address of their house with the nearest cross streets in case I panic and forget during a "crisis situation." In my three and a half years of baby-sitting for this family, I've never used the emergency list once—not even when Jamie was just a little baby and peed three times in one hour, or when Beth fell off her training bicycle and skinned her knee on the driveway. Not even when Lindsay told me I was a bitch for making her go to bed. Nevertheless, the list is always there waiting for me, every time.

Mr. Cooper returns to the kitchen with the gift. I hate it when the parents linger after they've picked me up, observing how I interact with the kids.

"Can we watch a video?" Beth says, with just a touch of whine in her voice.

I know Mrs. Cooper, who is getting her purse and coat from the front-hall closet, is still within earshot and not a big fan of "television as baby-sitter."

"Why don't you finish your dinner first, and then let's go up to the playroom and find a board game, and then we'll see how much time we have for videos before bed?"

It's a good answer. The Coopers kiss their kids good-bye on the tops of their heads—I've been here way too many times for any don't-leave-me-with-the-babysitter-crying crap. The shiny-pink wrapped gift from the bride and groom's registry is tucked safely underneath Mrs. Cooper's arm.

"Bedtime in one hour," she reminds us as they head out the door.

As soon as I hear the car rumble down the driveway, I turn back to the group and start using my real voice.

"Okay, here's the deal. I want everyone upstairs, teeth

brushed, pajamas on within ten minutes. If you get ready now, I'll let everyone stay up an extra half hour."

"What about—" Beth starts.

"No what abouts. This is the deal. Take it or leave it."

The kids eye one another for a few seconds and then push their chairs back and flee the room. I hear their feet bounding up the stairs before I've even cleared the plastic daisy place mats.

* * * * *

The Detroit area clubs' summer season culminates with the swim finals held at the end of July. The location rotates annually from club to club and every preceding meet serves as preparation for the final slaughter. The night before finals, we guards and coaches go to the houses of qualifying swimmers and vandalize their property. We are heavily armed with Kroger grocery bags stuffed with streamers in club colors, green and white, and paper-plate plaques, focusing on something positive, we have made for each competitor.

"Go, Backstroke Brenden! Swim Hard!"

"Shelly is Swelly! Freestyle to 1st Place!"

We empty can after can of menthol shaving cream; our hands are caked in the pastels of the sidewalk chalk we have worn down to small nubs and chunks. We declare our team the winner before any starter gun is fired, and toss toilet paper up into the blue-black sky, toward the thick branches of the decaying maple and elm trees. The rolls drop down with heavy, dull thuds, creating long white arms with nothing to hold on to, swaying despite the humidity.

This is tradition.

* * * * *

I've learned from experience that a visit to the fully stocked playroom within an hour of bedtime will get the kids way too hyper. Instead, I spread the Chutes and Ladders game on the floor of the den. It's where I spend the majority of my time after the kids go to bed and it's decorated just like the dens in most of my friends' homes: forest-green plaid pillows, a burgundy leather couch, and at least one wooden mallard duck sitting on a built-in dark-wood bookshelf. There's also a private bar higher up on the shelf, always stocked with enough variety to require an alcohol license, and always locked.

Sometimes the Coopers let me bring someone along if they're going to be out especially late, like on New Year's when I get paid double money. Last New Year's, Lucy and I found the key to the private bar in Mr. Cooper's cuff-link drawer.

We've taken sips from some of the bottles more than once.

In this town, three-o'-clock cocktails among the ladies come second only to the mandatory after-work drink among the men. The drinks are simple and classic—martinis, bourbon, scotch, straight up or on the rocks. I don't know how to make any of their favorite cocktails, like greyhounds or seabreezes. I just overheard the lingo when the Coopers had a holiday party and brought me over to keep the kids entertained.

I can hear the water running in the upstairs bathroom and Lindsay saying, "No, Jamie, you have to put the toothpaste ON the toothbrush," so I decide I have enough time to sneak a phone call to Lucy. She's baby-sitting for her cousin tonight and gave me the number, because it's family and it's always okay to call.

"Are they in bed yet?" she asks me.

"No—getting ready. Another hour. Yours?"

"Yeah. She's been out for almost forty-five minutes. She just sleeps all the time but I guess that's what you do at nine months."

"Lucky you," I say. "What are you doing now?"

"Sitting on the back porch smoking a cigarette."

"Damnit! I could never do that here. Lindsay could come down anytime and bust me." Just then all three kids walk into the room.

"You're not supposed to be on the phone," Beth declares.

"It's my MOM, smarty-pants," I lie. Lucy laughs and tells me to call her later.

The kids are all wearing flannel pajama sets and smell like mint. Lindsay's even brushed everyone's hair, including her own, and their blond tresses shine like a mirror catching the sun. The four of us settle in around the open board on the beige carpet, choosing our game pieces and rolling to see who goes first. I turn Nickelodeon on in the background but keep the volume down low so I'm not breaking my promise to Mrs. Cooper.

The headlights of the passing cars on the street sweep across the framed family photos on the wall, where Mr. Cooper stands with his beautiful wife and perfect children, smiling down on me. Over the years I've watched the number of pictures grow and sometimes I think if I could just remove a plant or rearrange a chair in the background, there'd be room for more than five within these snapshots—there'd be room for me.

Then Beth says, "It's your turn," so I roll the dice over the chutes and the ladders to see where I land and how long I can stay in the game.

* * * * *

It's the last meet of the season. We are victorious against our crosstown rivals from Bloomfield Hills, and everyone is in a celebratory mood. The fish flies have had their initial scraping for the night because, as the hosts of the meet, we also host the traditional post-meet dance. The deck by the deep end is converted to a dance floor. The DJ sets up near the guardhouse underneath a sturdy awning, protection from any rain showers that might creep into the Midwest summer evening.

The air is choked with chlorine as the eight-and-unders, bellies full of pizza and jacked out on pop, dance around in hyper, spastic circles. The eleven- and twelve-year-olds huddle in gender-defined clusters. The girls have painted their faces with their older sisters' makeup; the boys' necks are splashed with their fathers' aftershave. They're whispering about who Brenden will ask to "go with" him, their envious eyes burning holes into Shelly. The thirteen- and fourteen-year-olds brush off the DJ trying to play the "cool" songs. They roll their eyes and make declarations.

"This is so gay."

"I have my period."

"Like I can dance now."

The lifeguards and coaches gather near the parents, with lips puckered and noses brown.

The Lochmoor parents drink, asking for their sixth seabreeze or just one more martini, dry, signing the $60 or $70 tab to their house accounts and slipping the bartender a ten or a twenty. They wink, finger delicate pearl earrings, fidget with Rolexes, and suck olives off toothpicks.

The Lochmoor moms break away from their male counterparts to sneak cigarettes down at the shallow end of the pool. The long, skinny, white menthol sticks slither out from burgundy leather cases. The filters are quickly caked with fuchsia-rose lipstick twirled up from shiny black tubes with gold trim. They prop their cigarette-holding hand up with the other, cupping their tan and exfoliated elbows and taking long, deep drags, the smoke released slowly, like a whisper. They motion me over to their group, a cluster of chairs pulled up underneath an umbrella, hardly enough light in the dusk to see who is talking.

They pull me into their gaggle, their comments quick and overlapping little licks.

"You're doing such a great job with the kids."

"Are you having a good summer?"

"Ready for school yet?"

"Are the fish flies more than you can handle?"

They hold me tight until a Stevie Wonder song comes on and the Lochmoor moms release a collective squeal and rise from their flicked ashes. They grab my arm.

"Come on! We'll teach you how to do the electric slide!"

I do not know what that means.

Their mortified children clear the dance floor as the Lochmoor moms fall into several lines facing in one direction. I am wedged in between and forced to follow their movements.

Three side steps to the right.

Snap fingers.

Three side steps to the left.

Snap fingers.

Reach down to the floor with one hand.

Stand up and reach back behind me with the other.

Then kick to the right while turning to the left.

And repeat.

I do the same steps to all four sides until I've made a square. I am facing where I began and it looks exactly the same as when I started. And so I begin again.

The Lochmoor moms are teaching me how to be like them; how to be like each other, move in the exact same way, and create a consistent pattern. I fall into their formation, making boxes over and over again, repeating the steps until the song ends. And when it does, I am just another Lochmoor mom in training, standing around and waiting for something better to happen.

Chapter 9

The Things You Give Away

Lucy springs some news on me. She's decided to have sex.

It's a Tuesday afternoon during Grosse Pointe South High School's spirit week, and we're talking about our junior-class float—a giant king dressed in a South football jersey with the words "Purple Reign" spelled out below it, because as freshmen we voted purple our official class color. Someone even rigged up a jam box to blare the old Prince song (same name, different spelling) in the background. I get to ride in the parade on Saturday because I'm a class senator. Our convertibles come after those holding the homecoming court nominees of course. It's Stephanie DeMarco's third straight nomination.

"I bet I could get a dart blower and take out the wheels of Stephanie's car," I tell Lucy as we leave school, the hallways

113

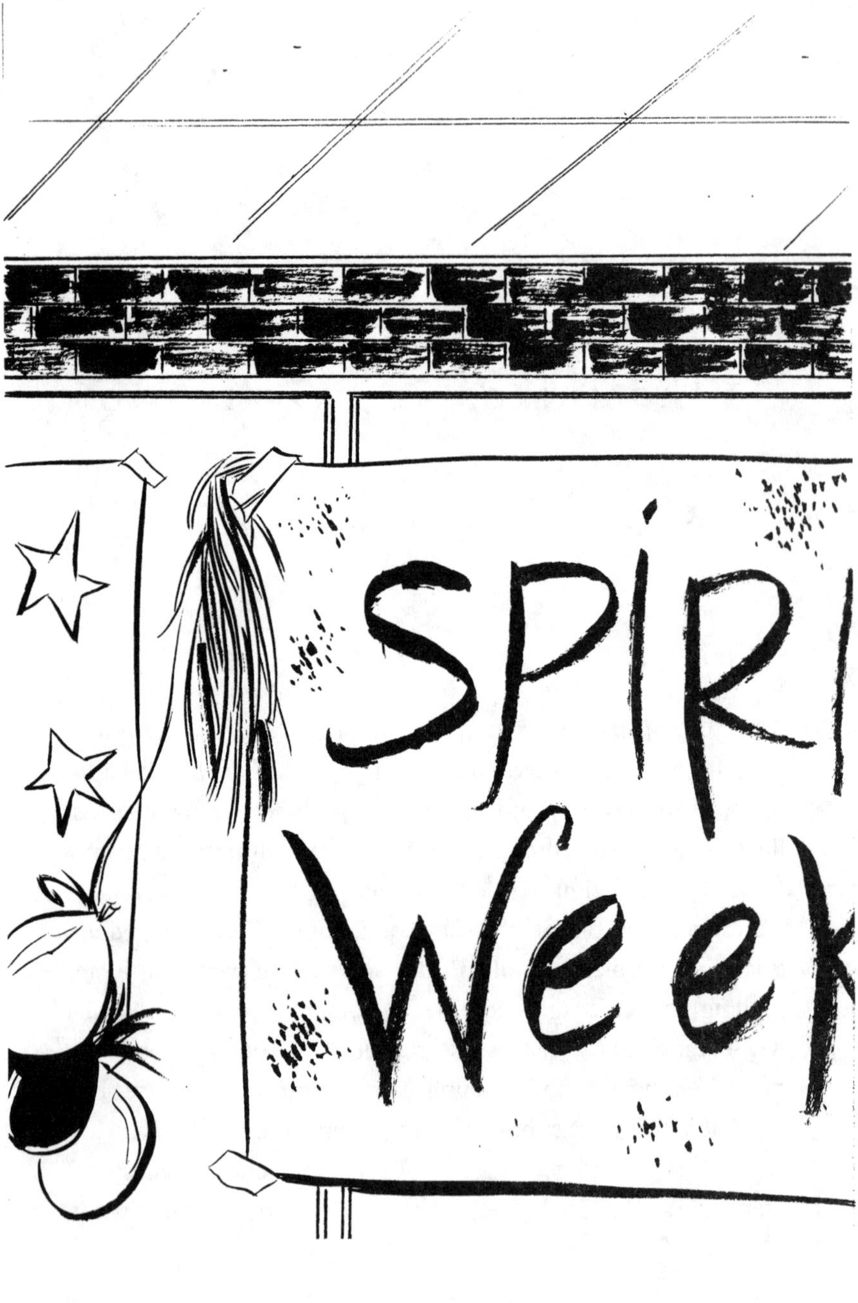
SPIRI
Weel

fluttering with glitter posters proclaiming "Seniors Rule!" even though their spirit day isn't until Thursday.

"I'm going to do it with Greg this weekend."

"What?"

I grab her arm and quicken our pace toward her car. Lucy has been going with the same guy for the last two years. Greg's older and graduated last June. He left to study business and economics at the state college an hour and a half away. He's been gone for about two months but comes home almost every weekend, including this one for the homecoming dance.

"I've decided." She unlocks the car doors and we slip inside for privacy.

"Why?"

"Greg's at college now. Those girls are way more sophisticated. Besides, I know he loves me." She flips down her visor to check her eye makeup. "After the homecoming dance, we're going back to his house. His parents are going to be out until at least one A.M. at some wedding at the yacht club. It's perfect!"

"Jesus," I say.

"We're sixteen now, Emma. I mean, some of the girls we go to school with have been doing it since eighth grade!" She turns the key in her ignition while I crack the window for my cigarette.

"Like who?"

"Katrina Krause."

"That's so not true," I say, surprised by my answer.

"Okay, what about Stephanie DeMarco and Brian Van Eden?" They're still going strong.

"Yeah, but she can get away with that kind of shit."

"Well, whatever. I don't want to go to college a virgin and we're seniors next year. Don't you sort of want to know what it's like?"

"I guess," I say, watching my reflection in her side mirror.

"What about Billy?" Lucy says.

"What do you mean, what about Billy? You know we're just friends," I tell her once again.

"Is that why you're going to homecoming together?" We're seven blocks from my house. I toss the cigarette out the window, spraying myself with perfume from my purse and unwrapping a stick of gum.

"We're going to homecoming as FRIENDS. Besides, he has a new girlfriend, some chick who goes to Star of the Sea. You know how he likes those Catholic-school girls."

"Whatever you say," Lucy smirks.

"I have someone else in mind."

"Oh yeah? Who's that?"

"Zack Thompson."

"ZACK THOMPSON? Are you high?"

"What? He's been calling me again."

"Of course he has," Lucy says, pulling into my driveway. She hates Zack because for the past three years, he's had this habit of calling me, getting together with me, and then dumping me for no reason and without explanation.

I have this habit of letting him.

One day we'll be at the movies making out in the back row, the next day his mom says he's taking the trash out and can he call me back? And he never does. He goes to the other high school, Grosse Pointe North, so he can do this and not have to contend with running into me in the hallways. Then anywhere from four to five months later he'll call me and the cycle starts all over again.

The cycle was most recently reset two weeks ago. It was too late to break the homecoming date with Billy, and besides, my best plan of attack with Zack seems to be pretending I don't give a damn.

"God, Emma," Lucy says, leaning over to give me the smoke-smell test before I go inside. "Zack Thompson? You should just throw yourself into the traffic on Mack Avenue."

★ ★ ★ ★ ★

Homecoming night, Billy Crandall puts on a tie and a sport coat and picks me up at seven P.M. The dance starts in thirty minutes. We're supposed to meet Lucy and Greg by the gym doors.

"You look great," he says, handing me a corsage box. I'm wearing the same black dress I wore to last year's homecoming. Dad's too pissed at Mom right now about her new boyfriend and, therefore, no new homecoming dress. He thinks her new boyfriend should buy it, she thinks he should stick it up his ass. Meanwhile, I'm recycling last year's semiformal wear, cleverly trying to disguise it with a shawl and different earrings.

"Why the hell did you buy me a corsage, you dork?" Billy laughs and helps me pin it on my dress.

When we get to school, we still have fifteen minutes left before meeting Lucy and Greg, so we pull into the church parking lot next door. Billy's got a forty-ounce Mickey's malt liquor in the front seat, next to a fresh carton of cigarettes.

"Why, Billy Crandall," I say in my best Tennessee Williams southern-belle accent. "If I didn't know better, I'd think you were trying to seduce me!"

He lights me a smoke and we pass the beer back and forth, still nestled in its brown paper bag. He's already loosened his tie.

"So tell me about Little Miss Star of the Sea," I say. "Is she freaking out because you're here with me tonight? You explained everything, right?"

"Nah, it's cool. It's nothing serious." He flips his black bangs back from his eyes. "So you talking to Zack Thompson again?"

"Fuck, did Lucy write up a story about it for the school newspaper?" I rest my heels on his dashboard.

"You sure you want to go down that road again?"

"There's no road," I say, smiling. "It's more like a cul-de-sac."

★ ★ ★ ★ ★

Lucy calls me the next morning after church. Her parents are in the kitchen and she shares her bedroom with her sister, so she sneaked out to the back porch for the debriefing.

"So how was it?"

"It was great." Her voice sounds small.

"Really?"

"Yeah," she whispers.

"How many times did you do it?"

"Twice."

"Really? Did it hurt?"

"Sort of but not really. You get used to it."

"Do you feel different?"

"I guess so."

"Like how?"

"Like—." I hear her screen door open. "Greg's here. I gotta go."

★ ★ ★ ★ ★

Mom corners me with the birth-control talk one afternoon after she catches me making out with Zack on our back porch. She'd been out on a date with Painter Nick. That's what me and my brother, Jack, call him because he runs a house-painting company. Mom met him at the hardware store two months ago. They went to a Lions game but left early because it was a total blowout, 42–3, the Lions losing per usual of course.

Zack and I had spent most of our Saturday wandering through the Village, eating grilled-cheese sandwiches at Claire-pointe restaurant. Fall was setting in and the air had started to outline our breath even when we weren't smoking cigarettes in the Jacobson's parking lot. Even though we were way too old, we headed for the swing sets at Maire Elementary School, behind Kroger's grocery store. Zack pushed me higher and higher, until I thought I was going to flip over the swing-set bars. I squealed and begged him to stop. When he pulled me down, we made out on the wood chips until I started worrying about who might be driving by. Our lips were sticky and sweet from my lip balm, our breath sharp with nicotine, when I pulled back and whispered, "Let's go to my house."

It takes only five minutes to get from the Village to our condo, but I'm too afraid to go inside without Mom there and decide it's not really breaking the rule of only having a boy over with a parent home if we just sit on the back porch. Zack kisses me mostly with his tongue and I'm so distracted by his boner pressing up against my jeans that I don't even hear Painter Nick's truck pull up. Zack quickly takes his hands out from underneath the back of my shirt, where they had been fiddling with my bra clasp.

We make the mistake of wiping our mouths as Mom and Painter Nick walk up, as if they need a reminder of what we've been doing. "Hello, Mrs. Harris," Zack says. He shakes her hand. Zack has an older brother who taught him how to sweet-talk the parents. "Hello, sir," he says to Painter Nick.

"Hello, Zack," Mom sighs. She's wearing a Lions hat that Painter Nick must have bought for her at the game. "Emma, we need to start dinner. You'd better head inside. Where's your brother?"

"Hell if I know," I tell her.

"Watch it," Mom says. Then in a sweeter voice, "See you later, Zack. Tell your mother I said hello."

"I will, Mrs. Harris."

Painter Nick just stands there in his canvas pants and T-shirt, smiling and holding the door open for Mom with dried splatters of taupe and navy blue in the creases of his hands. He's still in the "I'm your mom's special friend" phase, as if I don't know he spends the night here when I go over to Dad's. He leaves evidence all over our place—his razor on Mom's bathroom ledge, the grapefruit juice in the fridge that no one else would ever drink, his "Nick's Painting Co." sweatshirt left behind on the hook by the back door. A few weeks ago, one of Painter Nick's T-shirts even ended up in our laundry and ruined my favorite pair of jeans from the Express. Mom said it was an "accident" and I needed to "get over it." I told her maybe she needed to "get over" Painter Nick and she sent me to my room for the rest of the day.

I kiss Zack good-bye even though I know Mom is probably watching from the kitchen window. "Call you later," I tell him and wait until he's just a tiny speck down the street, on his skateboard, before coming inside.

Painter Nick is rinsing shrimp and sliding them onto skewers, then dipping them into some sort of marinade.

"We thought we'd cook out on the grill one more time before it really gets cold. What do you think?" He holds up one of the skewers like a baton.

"I think I'm not hungry," I say and go to my room, leaving Painter Nick standing there with brown sauce running down his fingers while Mom calls Tommy Mason's house to see if Jack's there.

Five minutes later, there's a knock at my door.

"Who is it?" I ask, holding the case to the mix tape Zack made me last week while it plays on my stereo. Track two is "Something to Believe In," my favorite Poison song.

"It's Mom. Can I come in?"

She sits on the edge of my bed. I concentrate on the tape case and Zack's handwriting and the picture of Perry Farrell he's pasted on the cover.

"I think we need to have a talk," she says.

"What? We weren't in the house, Mom, I swear!"

"I know that," she says. "I think we need to talk about birth control."

"Oh god, Mom, shut up! I am not having sex!" I bury my face in my pillow.

"Well, I know that. And just because I'm telling you about birth control doesn't mean I want you to go out and have sex."

"I don't even know what you're talking about." I refuse to look at her.

"I want you to be smart, Emma. I waited until I was twenty-one."

I've never heard this story before and it's worth sitting up for.

"So who was it?"

"A guy I worked with."

"Where is he now?"

"I have no idea. I never saw him after that night."

"Mom, what's the point of waiting until you were twenty-one if the guy ended up being a one-night stand anyway?"

"It wasn't a one-night stand!"

"Well, what was it then?"

"It was an . . . understanding." She takes the tape case out of my hand and places it on the nightstand. I can hear Nick making up his own song downstairs. It sounds like opera. He opens the oven door, then the refrigerator, then our cupboards he repainted three weeks ago. I imagine him pulling out plates and spices, as if he's lived here for years.

"Now," Mom says, her voice shaking. "Do you know how to use condoms?"

I think I might throw up.

* * * * *

"My parents are going out of town next weekend," Zack tells me. We're watching MTV together on the phone. I'm baby-sitting for the Coopers but the oldest kid keeps coming downstairs so it's too risky to have Zack sneak over for a visit.

"Oh yeah? Where are they going?"

"Up north to get the cottage ready for winter."

"Where are you staying?"

"Well, they think my brother is coming home from college to stay with me, but he's not."

"Hold on," I say, muting the Michael Jackson video and putting my hand over the receiver. I thought I heard the Coopers pull up in the driveway but it's just the next-door neighbors. "Okay. Go ahead."

"So, anyway, you think you might want to come over next weekend?"

"I think I'm supposed to go to some party with Billy . . ."

"Oh," he says. "Okay, whatever. Look, I should go."

"Wait," I say. I hear Zack tapping a pen in the background. "It's okay, I mean I'll just tell him something came up."

"Yeah?" Zack says, his voice all sweet again and gravelly.

"Yeah."

★ ★ ★ ★ ★

I make Zack lock the front and back doors even though his parents are six hours away. We take a bottle of Boone's Farm wine his brother scored for him up to Zack's bedroom. His bedspread is black and white striped. There's a Black Crowes poster on the wall and a pile of dirty clothes in the corner.

"Sorry," he says, passing me the bottle. "I should have cleaned up."

"It's fine," I say. I can feel him staring at me.

On his nightstand, I see the box of condoms, ribbed for my pleasure.

Later, when he's inside me, I hold my breath during the piercing pain and think about riding in the homecoming parade, the way I waved my hand to the little kids from the elementary school who lined the curbs, how adult and grown up I must have seemed.

It lasts less than a minute.

The empty wine bottle rolls on the floor next to us and stops with a thud against the wall.

The numbers on his alarm clock bleed 10:47 P.M.

I sit up and put my bra back on.

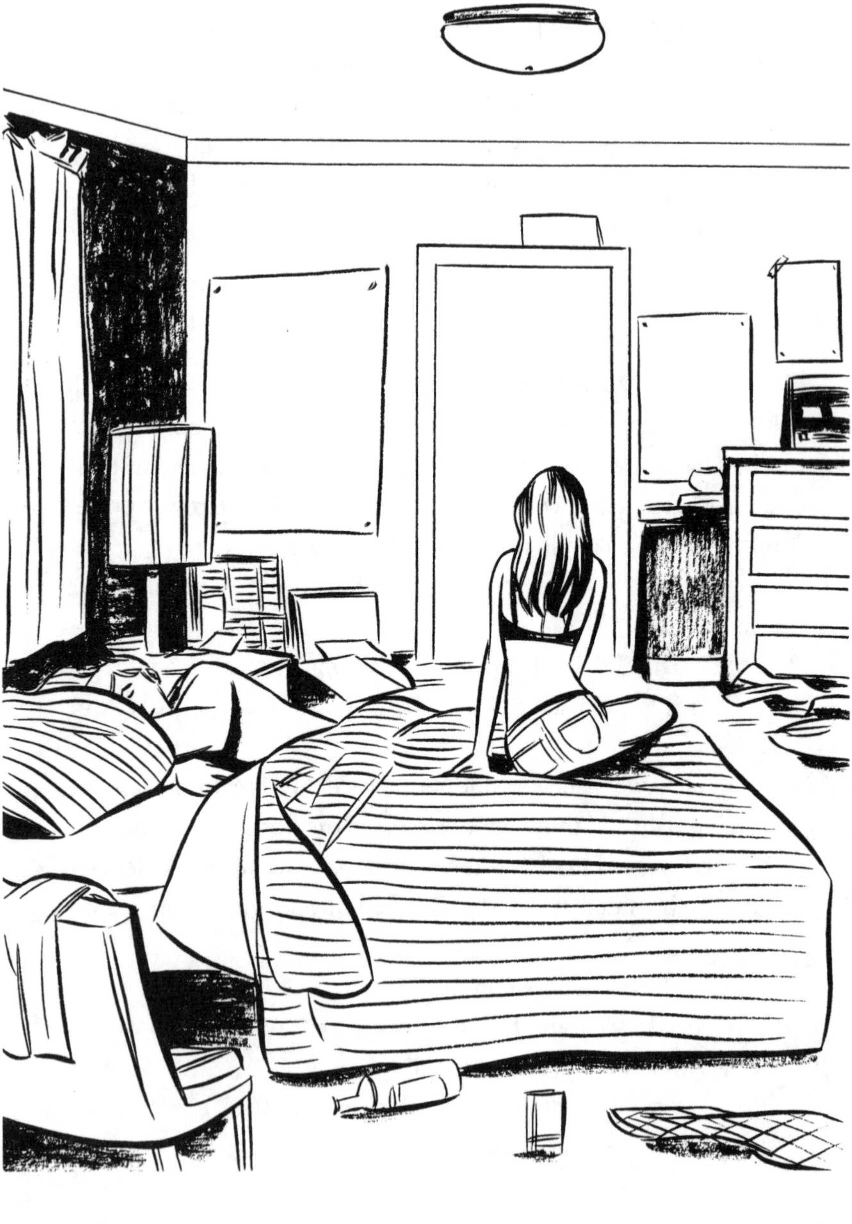

"I should probably go."

When he doesn't answer, I turn around to find him asleep, hugging one of his pillows, his mouth half open as if he wanted to ask me something but forgot what he was going to say.

⋆ ⋆ ⋆ ⋆ ⋆

Zack calls me the next day at 8:50 P.M. I have only ten minutes to talk before Mom's no-calls-after-nine rule, but for once I am grateful.

"What time did you leave last night?" he asks. There's a Red Wings game on in the background.

"Around eleven P.M."

"Oh. Sorry about falling asleep." I hear him flip to the Pistons.

"No big deal. I had to get home by midnight anyway. Curfew."

"Right." It sounds like he's chewing on potato chips. "So . . . you okay?"

"Sure," I lie. "So I'll talk to you after school tomorrow, right?"

"Right."

"Hey, Zack?"

"Yeah?" The chip bag rustles.

"Don't tell anyone. Okay?"

There's a long pause without words, just crackles like static and muffles and chews and then there's a gulp.

"Sorry. Had Ruffles in my mouth." Someone picks up the other extension at his house.

"Oh, Zack, would you come and take the garbage out for me?"

"Yeah, Mom," he says. There's a click. "Look, let me call you back."

"Don't worry about it."

★ ★ ★ ★ ★

Monday morning in between third and fourth period, Billy isn't waiting in our usual spot by the home ec classes. It's always been the easiest place to sneak out to the parking lot for our traditional smoke break. I find him already out in his car five minutes later.

"Where were you?" I ask, sliding into the passenger seat.

"Around," he says, taking a long drag. "Have a good weekend?"

His eyes are two hard rocks.

I don't answer. Instead, we sit in his car and let our third-period sociology class come and go, passing his cigarettes back and forth, our conversation nothing but puffs of smoke trying to form the words "I'm sorry" and "I know."

Chapter 10

Grosse Pointe Girl's Guide to Saturday Night

Ingredients:

Four friends, two of whom are still virgins. Two packs of cigarettes. Sixteen sticks of wintergreen gum. One mix tape marked "Spring Tunes—Junior Year." Four shades of lipstick: Moonlight Mauve, Kissing Koral, French Kiss, Cotton Candy.

One vehicle.

No destination.

Stir for approximately four hours. Repeat weekly for best results.

★ ★ ★ ★ ★

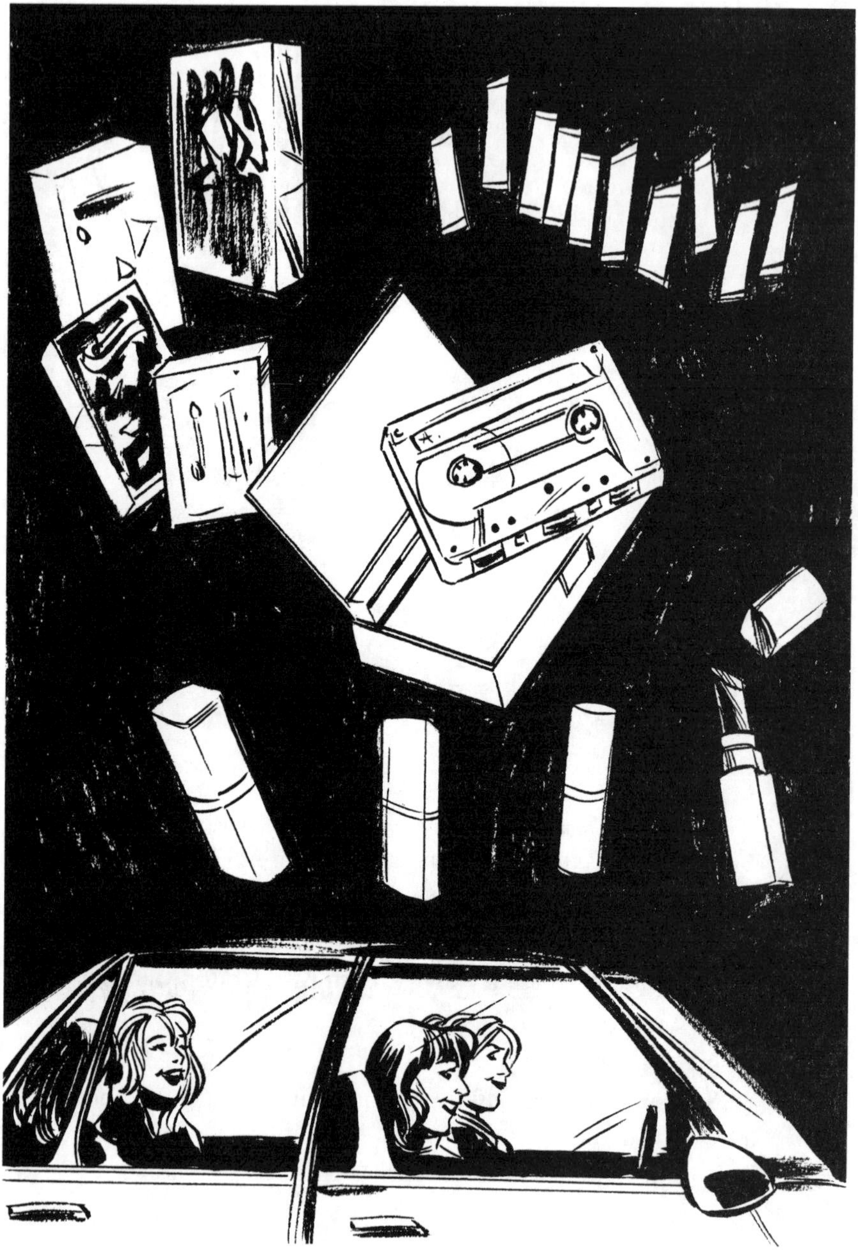

"Hold on a second, I want to take my other purse," Lucy says, bounding back up the stairs to her bedroom. "Other purse" is code for our secret stash of cigarettes. I hide mine rolled inside knee-highs in the back of my sock drawer. Lucy keeps hers tucked inside a wool hat buried in a shoe box, which is then stuffed underneath a pile of clothes in the bottom of her closet. She shares her room with her younger sister and has to be clever with her hiding places.

I sit opposite her mother at the dark-wood kitchen table and wait. A pot of homemade chili simmers on the stove.

"Would you like something to eat, Emma?" Lucy's mom asks, lighting a long, skinny cigarette. I fantasize about lighting up with her.

"No thanks, we'll probably eat something at the park." This is our phantom destination for the evening.

"How's your mother doing?"

"Oh, fine."

"And your father?"

"Fine," I say. "He has a new girlfriend. They're up north right now."

Through the kitchen window, I see Lucy's father in the garage tinkering with something on the lawn mower and smoking a cigar. Her brother sits nearby on a stack of bricks, feeding ridged potato chips to their mutt named Junior. Her sister wanders into the kitchen with the phone tucked between her shoulder and ear, pulling out the fixings for a peanut-butter-and-jelly sandwich.

Lucy's mom blows smoke through her teeth. "You girls should never start. It's a nasty habit."

She tells me this every weekend. I always respond the same way—a murmur that's not exactly a yes but not a definite no either.

It's why I always pick up Lucy first. With her family, there are no surprises.

★ ★ ★ ★ ★

Jennifer's out her front door before I finish pulling into her driveway.

"Hey," she says, sliding into the backseat with her long chestnut hair and turquoise eyes and freckles. I'm learning to accept the fact that she tortures boys without trying and I don't.

"What time do you have to be home tonight?" Lucy asks.

"Not until one. Fucking Asshole is out of town, so Mom's cool with it." Fucking Asshole is what Jennifer calls her father. It's the only time she swears.

I pick up Christina last. When we pull into her circular driveway, she's standing in the doorway having an argument with her parents. I can't hear what they're saying but Christina's eyes are extra large, like "Who, me?," and she's crossing her arms and shifting back and forth on her feet like she has to pee.

I roll down the window and smile at her parents.

"Come on, Christina, we should get to the park before it gets too late!" I throw this out for good measure.

Christina's park outfit consists of a purple miniskirt and matching tank top, large silver hoop earrings, and a stack of bracelets on her right wrist. Her quest for fashion is why she always gets grilled before making her escape.

"Who's going to be at the park?" her father asks in his thick Greek accent.

"Dad! I already told you!"

Her three younger sisters peek at my car from the living-room curtains, faces piled on top of one another like a totem pole.

"Just be home on time, Christina. I mean it," her mother says, finally relenting with a kiss on the cheek and a wave good-bye.

Christina pouts outside the front passenger door for shot-gun, but Lucy holds the position strong. Lucy smuggled the Dustbuster out of her house to erase our cigarette ashes, so she gets first choice, and first choice is always shotgun.

"Where are we really going?" Christina asks, settling in next to Jennifer.

"I heard Mike Cleveland's having a party," Lucy says.

"Yeah, but we don't really hang out with those people any-more, and besides, it's not like he invited us directly." I am always worrying about going where I am not welcome.

Jennifer, on the other hand, has no problem with proper Grosse Pointe etiquette. "Who cares? I'll go," she says, leaning toward the front to change the station on the radio.

"Hey! I liked that song!" Christina whines, wiggling in her seat. "Why don't we stop at Schettler's first and see what's going on?"

"Fine," I say. "I need more smokes anyway."

I make a right onto Lakeshore Drive.

★ ★ ★ ★ ★

Schettler's drugstore is ground zero. It serves as our start-ing and ending point on most weekend nights until the Grosse Pointe police shoo us away. The store sits directly across the street from the high school. Tonight, there are four cars parked outside. Stephanie DeMarco and her crew lean on the hood of her red Acura.

We do not wave.

Loitering around a Jeep Cherokee are the Huskies, a band of senior boys nicknamed for their uniform of Connecticut Huskies caps personalized across the back with iron-on letters. It's the Grosse Pointe version of a gang, except they're not really menacing, just terribly cute and for the most part not at all interested in us.

Christina has had a serious crush on one of the main Huskies, Tom Mason, for about three years now. He's tall, with sandy-blond hair and wet brown eyes, and he laughs at almost anything. He's one of the best swimmers in the school and I just spent a summer lifeguarding with him at the Lochmoor Country Club. Anytime we were on the same shift, I had to come home and immediately call Christina with a play-by-play. To me, he was just Tommy, the guard who stole my fries and burped in front of the girls and threw kids in the pool and put the lane dividers in for me during swim practice. To Christina, every detail was a clue, like did he ever talk about other girls and how did he react when I brought up her name and did he happen to say where he was going that night?

I was sort of secretly praying for Tom to get a girlfriend so Christina could move into the "Why? What's wrong with me?" phase and then the "He's such a dick!" phase and then we could just get on with it already.

Because we're not in any of those phases yet, and because I know she'll kill me if I don't, I call over.

"Hey, Tommy, what's up?"

He wanders away from his gang, toward our car, and leans on my driver's-side window.

"Hey, Emma," he says, and does the nod to the other girls. "You guys going to Spinners tonight?"

Spinners bar is our refuge in Canada where the drinking

age is only nineteen. This summer we finally got fake IDs from Bob's Photo, in downtown Detroit. The cheap imitations cost us $30 each but put us all somewhere between twenty-one and twenty-three. The bouncers usually let it slide because they know that Grosse Pointe kids practically finance their paychecks with $12 pitchers of beer.

"Yeah, maybe. I don't know," I tell Tom.

Christina kicks my seat.

"What are YOU guys doing?" I ask, Christina's invisible gun pointed at the back of my head.

"Probably going to Spinners," Tom says. He still has his summer tan and it looks even deeper against his yellow, button-down shirt.

I hear Christina hyperventilating behind me.

In the rearview mirror, I see Jennifer roll her eyes. She gets bored easily with boys. Her latest game is making us pull over so she can jump out of the car and pretend to faint on Lakeshore right as a cute boy is running by, just to see if he'll stop and help her.

Few do.

Lucy smiles at Tom politely, lights me a cigarette, and says nothing.

"Mike Cleveland was supposed to have a party but his parents came home early," Tom reveals.

"Oh yeah? I mean, yeah, we heard that," Christina offers from the back.

Tom's friends start honking the horn and shouting some weird Huskies chant.

"See you later," he says, and then, "'Bye, Christina!" with one of his perfect-teeth-thanks-to-Dr.-Barliatti smiles before walking away.

* * * * *

The traffic on the bridge to Canada crawls. I keep my eyes forward to try and forget we're hovering several hundred feet above the Detroit River.

"Yes, Christina," Jennifer says for the third time. "It probably DOES mean something if Tom said "bye' specifically to you."

Christina squeals at Jennifer's affirmation as we pull up to the border guard, handing over our real IDs. I run through the drill and give him the standard "We're going to Mother's restaurant for pizza" bullshit line in order to cross over.

The guard rubs his thick black mustache, examining our laminated licences.

I play with my bra strap peeking out on my shoulder.

He waves us through.

The Spinners parking lot looks more than half full, which is a good sign, and then we see some "Grosse Pointe South Lacrosse" stickers on the back windows of several cars, which is a better sign. It's 9:47 P.M.

"We're leaving by eleven-thirty," I remind everyone. "Right, Christina?"

"What?" she says, passing around pieces of gum wrapped in foil. "Okay, okay, eleven-thirty."

The bouncer tonight is a beefy brute with a mullet and a gold cap on his front tooth. We scoot toward him with our best smiles and chests pushed forward. Gold Tooth barely glances at our fake IDs tonight, just a quick scan with his flashlight followed by a stamp in the shape of a skull on our right hands.

Inside, our world metamorphoses into a cavern of dark red lights with neon purple borders. On the dance floor, a handful

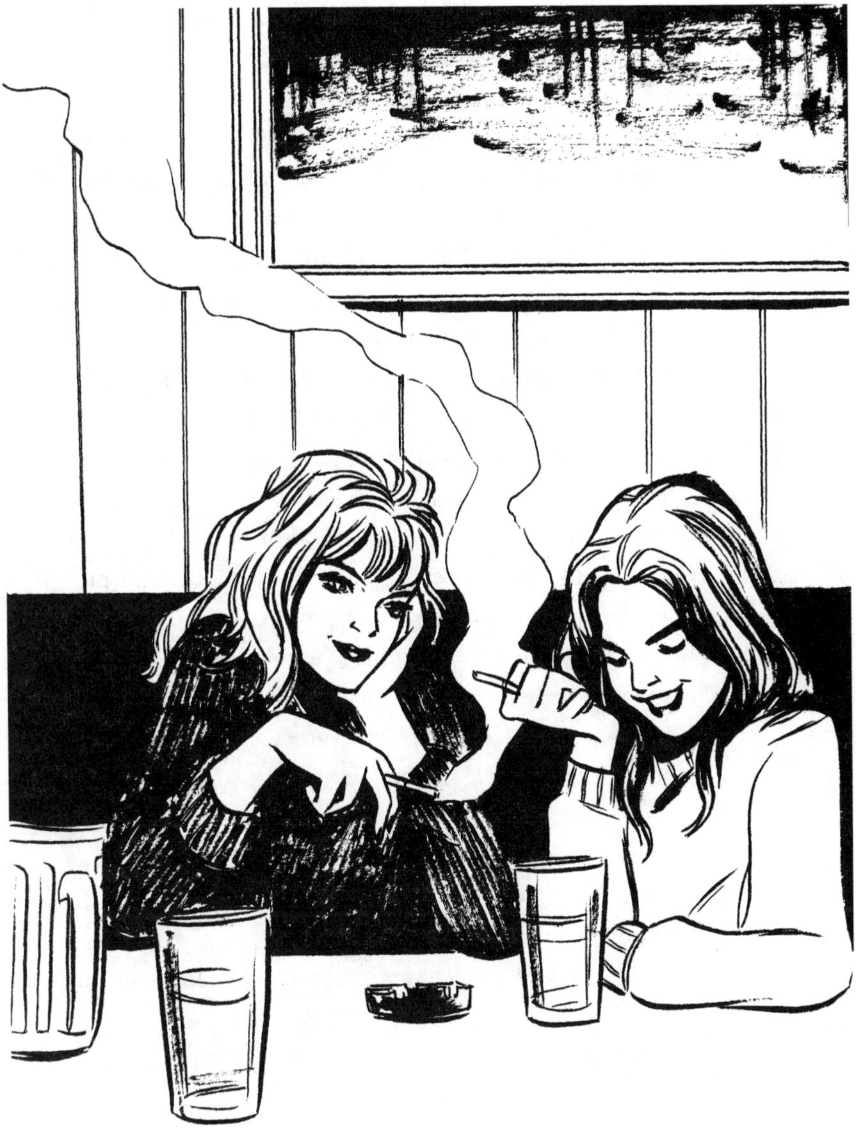

of my classmates pulsate to a Beastie Boys song, their faces captured in between strobe-light flashes, teenage bodies reflected in the mirrored walls.

I need a good buzz going before I can dance in front of people, let alone mirrors, so between the four of us, we buy two pitchers of beer, most of which Christina drinks.

"I just remembered, I didn't eat dinner!" she tells us in the middle of her third glass.

This of course means she's already drunk.

Mike's party must have been canceled after all, because he walks in with his group of friends, Todd and Tim and even Brian Van Eden, about thirty minutes after we do. Tom and his Huskies come in shortly after. Even with the mirrored walls, Spinners is small enough to get crowded easily, and within an hour Gold Tooth is holding the line at the door. Jennifer stands near our table nursing her beer and talking to a guy from her advanced placement chemistry class, ignoring his relentless, longing stare.

Christina keeps asking Lucy and me questions that don't really need answers while trying to keep an eye on Tom.

"There's a lot of people in here, huh?"

"It's loud in here, huh?"

"Who do you guys want to go to homecoming with?," which is just a cue to discuss whether or not Tom might ask Christina to homecoming.

My déjà vu sets in as Lucy and I smoke cigarettes end to end while we wait for a decent song.

"Aren't you tired of this?" I lean over and scream in Lucy's ear.

"Tired of what?" The DJ starts playing an oldie, "Come on Eileen," Christina's favorite. She grabs Jennifer from her lab partner and leads her out to the crowded floor.

"This. Spinners, or someone's lame party until the cops show up, and they ALWAYS show up. Or worse, we just drive back and forth between Schettler's and the St. Paul's parking lot, all night long, like we're looking for something."

I take a sip of my beer and in the mirror, watch Christina dance. Her moves consist of jumping around and tossing her hair and giggling while she waits for Tom to come near her. He's sequestered at the other corner of the dance floor with his Huskies, the back of his shirt slightly damp with sweat.

"We do the same thing every weekend."

"And?" Lucy asks.

"I don't know. It just feels like we're waiting for something to happen but nothing ever does. Nothing ever changes."

"And?" she says again.

★ ★ ★ ★ ★

The bar clock says it's 11:15 P.M., which really means it's eleven o'clock. Our beer is watery and we're down to one $10 bill.

"Where's Billy tonight?" Jennifer asks, dabbing the tiniest trace of sweat off her brow with a cocktail napkin. Christina's still on the dance floor working her way through Kurt Cobain's angst.

"I don't know, at his girlfriend's probably."

"Who is it this time?" Lucy asks.

"Julie? Jodie? Joanie? I forget. She's a Regina girl." It's one of the area Catholic schools.

"What does she look like?" Jennifer asks.

"What do they all look like? Blond, petite, rake."

Jennifer and Lucy share a snort giggle.

"What was that for?" I ask.

"Nothing."

"What?"

"It's just so obvious," Jennifer finally says. "He keeps picking anyone who is the exact opposite of you."

"I think that's what he really loves," I tell them, sprinkling my ashes on the heap of stubbed-out butts. "The things I'll never be."

★ ★ ★ ★ ★

By eleven-thirty, the crowd is mostly a bunch of kids who graduated last June and haven't left for college yet. If we leave now, we can make it back in time to stop and eat at the Ram's Horn in Grosse Pointe. It's open twenty-four hours and they don't serve alcohol, just food that's ordered from a menu in pictures and a $2.50 minimum per person.

Tom and his friends are still here, providing our greatest challenge—getting Christina to leave before he does. She likes to pinch when she's drinking, and also dash off and hide, so it takes some effort to actually get her out of there. As we're walking out the door, I see Tom in a back corner booth talking to Cathy, another girl in his class. She has her hand on his knee and keeps whispering in his ear, and it's a good thing Christina already raced to the car for shotgun because I do not want the "Why not me?" phase to start on the way home.

★ ★ ★ ★ ★

On the way back over the bridge, we run through the usual exit scene. This time, the guard is a woman, her hair so tight in its bun that her skin looks like a mask stretched over her bones.

"How long have you been in the country?"

"Just a few hours," I answer, chewing gum feverishly.

"What was the nature of your visit?"

"We went to Mother's for pizza."

She pauses, looking at my driver's license. "Why didn't you take the tunnel back? It's closer to Mother's."

I freeze.

"Traffic," Jennifer offers from the back. "It was really bad."

"Okay. Have a nice night," she says.

At Ram's Horn, we pool what remains of our baby-sitting and allowance money. It's just enough to meet the Ram's Horn minimum but doesn't include a tip. We dig through our purses to come up with another two dollars in change. The Ram's Horn waitresses have to wear brown uniforms with cream-colored maid aprons and black orthopedic shoes over nylons. Leaving even just a little extra something seems like the right thing to do.

Lucy and I order coffees and fries to split, and Jennifer and Christina finally agree on the chocolate cake. There's a Muzak version of "On the Wings of Love" playing and it makes Christina weepy. She fidgets with sugar packets until the cake comes, and then dips her finger into the frosting, licks it, and repeats until Jennifer tells her to knock it off.

Eating our meal we are startled by a crash followed by a shriek. The Ram's Horn waitress has dropped her glass coffee pot, the brown liquid a steaming pool on the floor around her thick shoes, shattered glass making red dots of blood in her calves. The manager comes over in his skinny black tie. Instead of asking if she's okay, he shakes his head like he's calculating how much it'll cost to replace the broken pot.

"What a jerk," I say, swirling my fry in ketchup.

"Yeah, but at least we saw something different tonight, right?" Lucy says.

I shrug.

It's 12:14 A.M. We still have ashes to vacuum and drop-offs to make, so we leave a ten-dollar bill, four quarters, six dimes, five nickels, and fifteen pennies on the table, wave to the waitress, and head out the door.

Chapter 11

Unexcused Absences

Twenty-two days before senior prom, Mike Cleveland walks into the garage of his parents' home armed with his older brother's Pink Floyd tape and an opened envelope from Yale University. On the desk in his second-floor bedroom sits a neat pile of acceptance letters from several colleges—University of Michigan, Penn State, and even Notre Dame. The spring air sneezes into the room through the window that faces east, causing the letters to flutter from the oak wood onto the plush blue carpet.

Mike slides behind the steering wheel of his dad's brand-new black Cadillac. He fastens his seat belt and locks the doors, because it's what his mother would want him to do.

Then he turns the key in the ignition.

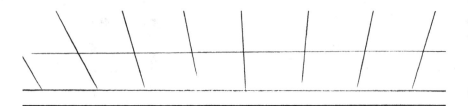

The song is "Comfortably Numb."
The Yale rejection letter rides shotgun.

★ ★ ★ ★ ★

The next morning during first-period journalism, the voice of our principal comes on overhead, seeping into the classroom like smoke from what will become a four-alarm fire.

He pauses to clear his throat.

We wait for a reminder about the Mothers' Club spring flower sale or a warning of the consequences of missing school on the unofficial senior skip day.

The PA system is temperamental and delivers his words in bits and pieces, like a telegram.

"Over the weekend . . ."

The teachers pull the shades on the windows.

"Tragic accident . . ."

They stand guard near the door.

"Mike Cleveland, a senior . . . died."

Three desks behind me, Megan Hunter breaks into tears.

"He was my prom date," she manages between her tornado-siren wail.

★ ★ ★ ★ ★

By third period, the decision is made to cancel classes for the rest of the day. Our teachers inform us that the counselors will remain on campus in case anyone wants to talk about the accident.

I find Lucy in the main hallway making a collect call from the pay phone to her boyfriend Greg's college dorm room.

"It's so awful," she sobs. "We've all known him since sixth grade."

I hover and stare at my shoes. My left lace is untied. I leave it that way.

"Can you come for the weekend?" she begs Greg. I give her a half wave and decide to find another method home. My legs move at 33 rpm through the student body, a mass of zombies around me emitting low buzzes of partial words.

Billy Crandall is leaning against my locker, waiting.

"You need a ride?" he asks.

My eyes burn for the first time since the news broke.

"Thank you," I mouth as he enters my combination for me. "Thank you."

* * * * *

The memorial service is announced for Saturday at St. Paul's. Through the rest of the week, word spreads quietly in the halls of a rendezvous Friday night at the church parking lot. The cars begin to gather after dark and line up next to each other in neat rows on the edge of the adjacent elementary school playground. Headlights are left on, casting shadows on the empty jungle-gym bars, equipment we outgrew years ago.

In the distance, the house where the priests sleep remains dark.

The Grosse Pointe police keep their distance, for once.

We begin in our familiar groups. I'm with Lucy, Christina, Jennifer, and Billy of course. Cases of beer litter the pavement. Some keep their cans protected in blue foam cozies printed in white with the logo and phone number of a landscaping company. Our tongues grow thick with each sip. We stop caring about lines and rules and break away from our usual clusters, morphing free-form into others.

Stephanie DeMarco asks, "Can I bum one of your Marlboros?"

I nod and prepare to light it for her.

"That's okay, I can do it myself," she says, taking it from my fingers.

We take each drag of our cigarettes as if it's our first, our last, letting the smoke fill our lungs, holding on to it for as long as possible.

Billy and Brian Van Eden ad-lib lines from *Caddyshack* and *Breakfast Club*.

Lucy describes her prom dress to Stephanie.

Todd Anderson and I discover we're going to the same college next fall.

No one talks about tomorrow.

My watch reads midnight as Katrina Krause pulls up with her group of friends. We make eye contact but say nothing. Instead, I blink away the "I miss you" I've been holding on to for the last four years.

From Brian Van Eden's truck come the strains of an old U2 song. "Want to slow dance?" he announces, grabbing Stephanie around the waist, her arms straight on his shoulders like it's eighth grade and the chaperones are watching.

We cheer at their demonstration from a time when everything made sense.

I let Billy Crandall keep his hand on the small of my back the entire night, guiding me between the smell of cheap beer and nicotine to remind me that I'm still here.

★ ★ ★ ★ ★

In the last year of middle school, when we were deemed old enough to take home our own report cards, finding out each other's grades was a game of truth or dare. No matter who asked Mike his grade-point average, he would say, "3.0."

I knew he was lying.

"What did you REALLY get?" I'd scrawl on my notebook in homeroom, trying to make my handwriting look cool with bubbles and circles, hearts above the *i*'s.

"3.9. Don't tell anyone," he'd respond, passing the book back.

I never did.

We wanted the same thing: to be just like our friends.

★ ★ ★ ★ ★

My alarm goes off at eight on Saturday morning. I wake up in a haze from the night before, remembering that I broke curfew but not caring about the repercussions. Soon I will be getting ready for prom but today I dress as if for Sunday mass: black skirt below the knees, stockings, and sensible shoes.

The sky is cement and soot.

At noon, I pull up to St. Paul's in my parents' car with the Girls by my side. We've borrowed our mothers' clutch purses and stand with arms crossed over our chests, shivering. In Michigan, the weather likes to turn without warning.

We should have worn sweaters.

The lot is full of SUVs and luxury sedans, cars that are sleek and washed and waxed, a brigade of dark colors and chrome wheels. Most arrive in even groups of two, four, six, but then there are those like Billy Crandall who insist on arriving alone.

When we gather inside the church, there's no casket or large framed portrait. There's not even an urn of Mike's cremated ashes.

There's no sign of a body.

* * * * *

The pews are solid pine, rigid on our backs and tailbones. I used to think they were built that way as a means of forcing me to pay attention whether or not the sermon was delivered with flair. I file in next to Billy. Lucy and Greg follow, with Jennifer and Christina at the end. In front of us a sleeve holds the hymnal, the Bible, small pencils and offering envelopes, because prayers alone cannot buy starched white robes, thin wafers, or candles for remembrance.

I study people from the back, looking for familiar details. The boys I have known since Brownell wear their sport coats and khakis left over from homecoming. It's been just over six months since then but the clothes seem to hang on their frames, as if their bones have shrunk. They sit together, their hair shaved evenly on their necks.

For the first time, I notice how things have changed, like Brian Van Eden is finally taller than Tim Osborne.

Mike used to be the tallest of them all.

Stephanie DeMarco anchors the girls' end of the pew, her hair still wonderfully curly and endless even in a crisis situation.

We hold cream-colored programs with an illustration of the church on the front, the interior text printed in simple Times New Roman. We are constantly referring to these booklets as a means of determining what comes next.

"Mike Cleveland," we read across the top. There are dates

underneath his name, beginnings and ends. At some point, every girl in my class practiced writing "Mrs. Mike Cleveland" in her diary. I want to take one of the miniature church pencils and make a correction.

★ ★ ★ ★ ★

Once I find the Cleveland family in the front pew, I can't take my eyes off them. They sit in their grief with perfect posture.

Three people are scheduled to speak for the family—boys who have known Mike since age five, ten. They speak about him in the present tense, their words varying only slightly.

Todd Anderson says, "He is like a brother to me."

"He is a brother to me," Tim Osborne says.

Brian Van Eden takes the podium last.

"He is my family," he says, his voice cracking.

I watch Brian Van Eden begin to cry and immediately forgive him for all past acts of cruelty.

My own tears feel like a second skin, a layer of makeup, a breeze off the lake. They are hot and quiet, slippery and silent. They drip off the edge of my chin, below my cheekbones, my jawline, a slight tingling sensation in my eyes. Billy wipes them away with his broad fingers and then clasps them in my own.

"This isn't supposed to happen here," I whisper, my breath shallow and increasingly fast.

I fix my gaze on the hymnal board, memorizing the numbers: 429, 470, knowing very well my lips will not move again as the others hold on to their books, singing in light voices, wavering, unsure, as the organ player tries to lead us to the bridge.

* * * * *

After the service, we gather at the Cleveland house. The kitchen counter is stacked with casserole dishes. There's no room left in the refrigerator for the trays of lasagna, spinach quiche, rolled beef enchiladas with Spanish rice, Swedish meatballs, turkey loaf, chicken divan, mashed potatoes, broccoli with cheddar cheese and bread crumbs, thick stew in a CrockPot.

There are enough meals to last at least a month.

"Why do people always bring food to funerals?" I ask Billy.

"I don't know," he says, loosening his tie. "Same thing happened at my dad's service. I guess it's hard to remember how to do normal things, like eat. It's just easier if some things are laid out for you."

We wander through the rooms. There are framed pictures of Mike on every coffee table—Little League uniform, Halloween costumes, varsity football pose.

A white sheet cake sits on the dining-room table without an inscription. It's like we're throwing him a surprise party but he hasn't shown up.

"Do you want to get out of here?" Billy asks, reading my mind.

* * * * *

The first day back to classes, I go to my counselor, Mr. Pearson. It seems there's been a unanimous decision to phase out the open-grief sessions.

"It's better to move on and not think about sad things. You kids have your whole lives ahead of you," Mr. Pearson tells me.

He's a wiry man who always wears brown cardigan sweaters. "Prom is in just a couple of weeks! Won't that be fun?"

I nod and leave for my second-period class, Spanish III.

Mike's seat, first row, last desk in the back, remains empty.

"Hola," Señor Thomas says.

"Hola," we respond, opening our textbooks to where we left off. This week, we learn to conjugate the verbs *"bailar,"* which means "to dance," and *"salir,"* which means "to leave."

* * * * *

I still see Mike sometimes, when I sleep.

Tonight, we are in his living room, his parents seated on the couch across from us. Stephanie DeMarco and Megan Hunter and Kelly Davis are in the kitchen making dinner. They do not seem to notice or mind that I'm here. They laugh, pulling out too many pots and pans. There are good smells making their way through the house, pot roast and a cake baking. Over the touchdowns of a college football game playing in the den, the steady whir of a handheld blender whips frosting made from scratch.

It feels like a Sunday.

Mike and I are trying to have a very sensible discussion with his parents to explain why. I can't make out his exact words but it feels like I'm on his side. I remain calm and want to hold his hand but we're sitting in separate armchairs.

"Dinner is ready," Stephanie calls from the kitchen.

The timing is right. It seems as if everything that needs to be said has been said. We all stand, as if we've made an agreement or come to a conclusion. I know Mike isn't going to stay for the meal, but I don't point this out to his parents. We all sort of squeeze each other's arms, the closest we can come to a group hug. His parents exit to help the girls set the table.

I stay behind.

"I should have kissed you," I tell him.

"When?" he asks.

"At the Farms Pier. I liked you, I was just afraid."

"It's okay."

"I'm sorry."

"It wouldn't have made any difference."

When he hugs me, I can smell the apple pectin shampoo he washed his hair with. He's wearing his reading glasses from eighth grade.

His heart beats against my own, still alive.

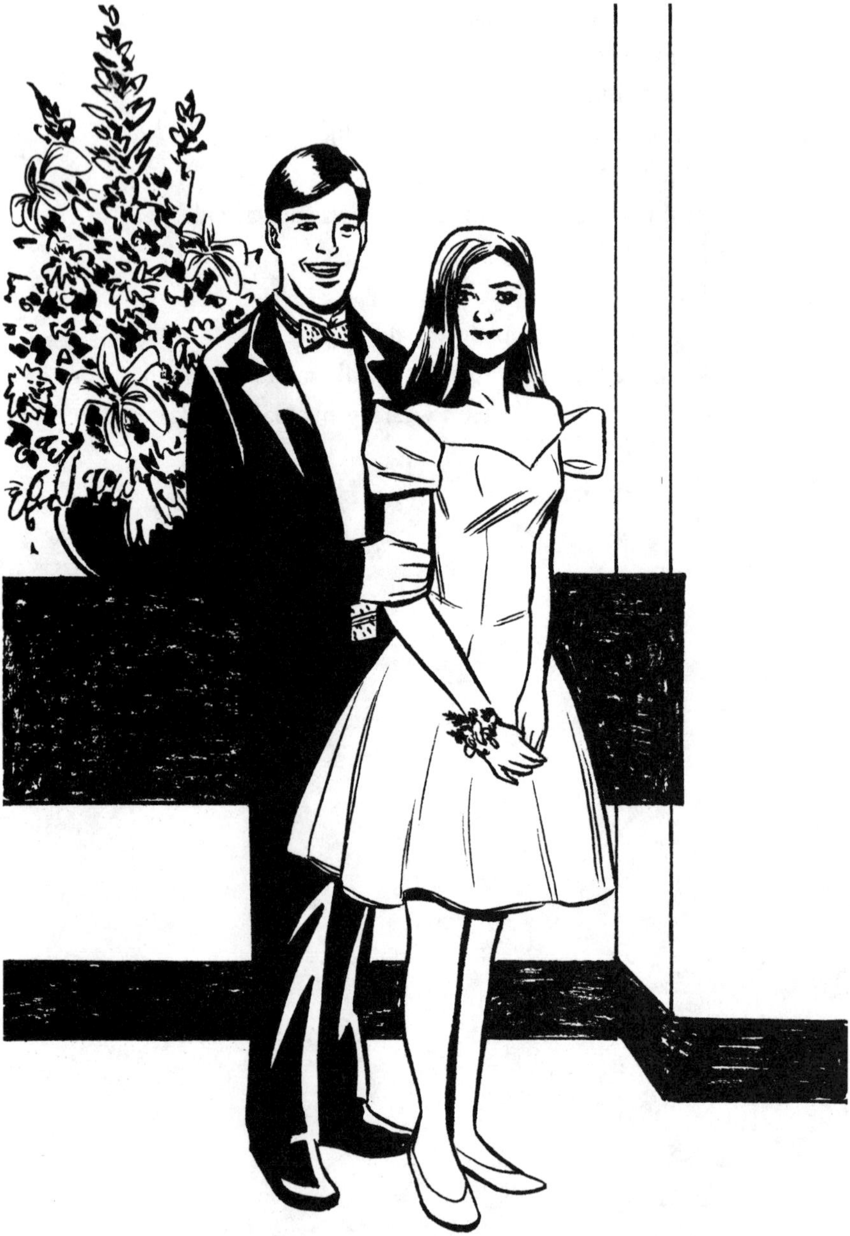

Chapter 12

Prom and Circumstance

"Yellow?" I say to Mom as if she's committed a crime, holding her prom photo in my hands. She stares back at me from twenty-five years ago in a chiffon dress that teeters around her waist like a bell. Her hair is a golden helmet, her hands gloved in white. The boy with his crew cut, standing next to her, smiles, his pants several inches too short.

"That was the style back then," she says, folding laundry in the living room.

"You look like Peggy Lee." I giggle.

"If you're just going to sit there and make fun, give it back."

The phone rings, buried underneath a pile of white cotton sheets and lavender towels. Mom passes it to me.

"Hello?"

"Hey." It's Lucy. "I just found my prom dress!"

"What does it look like?"

"It's yellow."

I pause. "Wow, really? Yellow. That's cool."

Mom throws the *TV Guide* at my head.

* * * * *

"Emma, it's time to make a choice."

I'm standing behind the locked door of the Lord & Taylor dressing room. We've been here for three hours, zipping up selection after selection. My hair is knotted on top of my head, my makeup worn off. I try to picture straight and smooth locks blown dry professionally and the matte-red lips and smoky gray eyes Mom has promised me.

"Give me a second!" I bark back at her. It's been over twenty minutes since I last let her in but I've managed to narrow the candidates down to three. Number one is dark magenta, floor length, with spaghetti straps. Number two is a three-quarter-sleeve V neck in black with a rhinestone-accented hem that hits at the knee. The final option is white silk, off the shoulder, with a full skirt supported underneath by a lace crinoline.

Lucy's boyfriend, Greg, is already back from his first semester at the University of Michigan. She is, of course, going away to the same school in the fall. His fraternity brother Pete agreed to be my date, making it a foursome.

"I'm a little surprised you're not going with Billy," Mom said to me again this morning on the way to the mall.

"Mom, is it that hard to accept that a guy and a girl can just be friends?"

"So, go as friends then."

"Billy's taking his GIRLfriend."

"Well, whoever she is, she won't look as good on his arm as you."

I rolled my eyes but secretly prayed that she was right.

I try to picture snapshots of the upcoming event. Like Mom's yellow disaster, my selection will be frozen in time. I think about cutting Pete out of the photos after they're developed, inserting my date of choice depending on my mood.

"That's right," I'll tell my kids someday. "Your mommy went to the prom with the Red Hot Chili Peppers." And then they'll look at me the same way I look at Mom when she talks about Creedence Clearwater Revival.

I pick up the white dress once again, slipping it over my body. If I had a bouquet of flowers in hand and a veil, I might pass for a bride.

Maybe it'll make Billy Crandall want to marry me.

I turn the door lock. Mom is slumped in a chair, digging through her purse for a mint.

"I choose this one."

"Are you sure it's what you want?"

Not really, I think. But it will do.

★ ★ ★ ★ ★

On the weekend before the big day, Lucy and I race around the Village gathering the final touches.

"Remind me again why we're not taking a limo like everyone else," I ask her while we're in Jacobson's picking out nylons. I'd never been in a limousine before and had been looking forward to the miniature TV, hoping people on the street would think we were rock stars when we passed by.

"We don't need one. Pete's parents bought him a brand-new Beamer for doing so well first semester."

"A Beamer?" I say, reading the size chart on the back of the Hanes package. "My parents bought me a frozen yogurt the first time I got a B plus in gym."

"Emma, come on, I'm serious. We're going with college men!" Lucy said too loudly on purpose. "Not those stupid boys from our class. I'm so sick of them."

"Right," I say, and imagine Billy Crandall in his beat-up Turismo and the cupcake date who will be sitting in my place.

* * * * *

Fraternity Pete pulls into my driveway in his silver present with his Greek letters tattooed to the rear window. Lucy and Greg are waving frantically from the backseat.

"We are going to have the BEST time," Lucy squeals as she hops out of the car.

"Hello, Emma, you look great," Pete says, shaking my hand like we've just met. He might in fact think that's the case. The last two times I've seen him at U of M parties, he was so drunk he called me Anna for most of the night.

He hands me a wrist corsage.

"Thanks," I say.

Mom snaps candid photos.

It's exactly what I expected—a red rose nestled in baby's

breath on an elastic band. The local florists must crank them out like assembly-line workers during this time of year.

Mom poses us first inside in front of the fireplace mantel, then switches our background to underneath the blossoming lilac tree. It rained earlier in the day and my white satin heels sink into the soft ground. She insists we take one of our large green golf umbrellas in the car with us in case the storm returns.

"You don't want to ruin your dress," she reminds me, as if I plan on wearing it again. "Be safe," she says, her eyes tearing up.

"Mom, knock it off." I slide into the front passenger seat. The Beamer still smells like a new car. It even has a CD player.

"Isn't this nice?" Lucy says from the back, practically on Greg's lap in her yellow gown. She looks like a stick of butter.

"Very nice," I tell her, keeping my promise to be polite. I look over at my date. He's mouthing the words to the Boyz II Men song playing on the radio. Billy sings along with this song too, but he does it in a high falsetto until I beg him to stop.

Fraternity Pete looks like he's in serious pain with every verse.

I bet he uses terms like "make love." I wonder if it works with sorority chicks.

He catches me looking at him and winks.

Yep, I think, trying to maintain my fake smile. It probably does.

* * * * *

The senior class was able to raise enough money to hold the prom in downtown Detroit at a fancy reception hall usually reserved for weddings. We ride a long escalator up several stories, overlooking a waterfall. At the entrance, we're handed key-chain replicas of our tickets and directed to a fake flower arrangement for our professional photo. Later, they will be delivered in a cheap plastic frame with the words "Together Forever—Senior Prom" painted in gold lettering across the bottom.

Our place settings are right next to Stephanie DeMarco's eating-disorder table, where she and her girls move the food around on their plates but never actually raise a fork to their mouths.

Billy sits a few tables back. He salutes me from across the room as I take my seat. I nod my thank-you.

During the main course of chicken cordon bleu, Lucy and I debate the awards ballots tucked underneath everyone's coffee saucer. We have until dessert to turn them in. Stephanie and Brian are a lock for prom king and queen, but at least we still have a voice in best dressed. Stephanie and her girls are all wearing the exact same dress in a variety of sherbet shades. The open backs expose a crisscross of faint strap lines, evidence of the girls' prep time at the tanning salon.

So far, I'm the only one wearing white. This is not necessarily a good thing.

"What about Katrina?" Lucy suggests, motioning across the room toward the bathroom where the girls gather every fifteen minutes to check for runs in their stockings. Katrina has just come out and breezes across the room in a black sheath that hugs her body, her neck wrapped in a white chiffon scarf, hair meticulous in an updo with a small butterfly rhinestone clasp at the base. She looks like Grace Kelly.

"Yes," I say, spelling out her name on the paper.

"You sure you're okay with that?" Lucy asks.

"Of course. It was a hundred years ago. It's not like I hate her or anything."

Fraternity Pete starts telling another "really funny story" about a new pledge who threw up all over the house pool table. I smile and toss my hair and place my hand on my date's arm as if I'm having the best time ever.

I wonder if Billy Crandall is watching.

"Whoo," Fraternity Pete says, wiping away the tears of laughter from his eyes. "That WAS a time." And then, "Yo, I gotta pee."

Charming, I think, but I'm grateful for the reprieve.

As soon as he's out of sight, I tell Lucy, "Be right back," and get up before she can ask for more details. I spot Billy on the crowded dance floor and make my move while his latest Catholic girl has her back turned requesting a song from the DJ.

We have less than a minute. He touches my shoulders briefly as I pass, pulling me slightly closer.

"We are here with the wrong people," he whispers.

It's not opinion but fact.

With my lips against his ear, I breathe a hot and quiet reply. "I know."

And as quickly as we come together, we separate before anyone sees us holding on, like leaves you keep trying to rake into one pile only to have them blown apart by an unexpected wind.

After four years, it has become clear. This is the only way we work: brief dramatic flashes, beautiful but too brilliant to stare at for too long.

★ ★ ★ ★ ★

The Monday after the prom, the highlights circulate rapidly. Tim Osborne's after party at the downtown Omni got busted at two A.M., but his father, having sanctioned the gathering with his own credit card, made one phone call to the front desk. The security guards promptly apologized and told the group to have a good night. Megan Hunter drank three bottles of Boone's Farm wine on her own and started crying hysterically about Mike Cleveland, apparently revealing that she had just had sex with him for the first time only weeks before he'd taken his life. Chris Bailey pulled into his driveway after dropping his date off and didn't set the parking break all the way. His parents' Mercedes was discovered the next morning on the front lawn, wedged against an elm tree.

Our night was not nearly as eventful. Lucy's parents left us alone in her rec-room basement where we watched scary movies and disguised shots of peppermint schnapps in our hot chocolates. By the time she and Greg went in the other room to "do laundry," Fraternity Pete had already passed out. As I watched Jason whack another busty camp counselor at Crystal Lake, I slipped the corsage off my wrist, placed it next to my date's head, and decided there might be a God after all.

By Tuesday, the hallway buzz has turned from prom to graduation, just a week or so away. I'm thankful for the subject change, hoping to avoid shared details of Billy's prom night. We've reinstated our traditional third-period smoke break in his car. This week, the hall monitors don't even bother asking us for passes when we saunter into class fifteen minutes late.

"Are you ready?" Billy asks me, rolling down the window. "Do you know what you're going to say?"

I've earned the distinction of commencement speaker after

auditioning with twelve other students. My speech, "The Road to Oz," is packed with analogies and lessons: the yellow brick road being the path ahead of us; the quest for a brain, a heart, and courage; ruby-red shoes that gave you the power to control your destiny the entire time.

I had no idea what I was talking about. The administrators ate it up.

"Sure. I'm going to tell three hundred and fourteen people what to do with their lives."

★ ★ ★ ★ ★

The night before graduation, Billy Crandall and I drive over to the school grounds around midnight. The front lawn has been set up for the event, and if the weather holds, tomorrow at seven P.M. we will begin our walk across the stage in front of the blue-and-gold banners and accept our diplomas and wonder what comes next.

Billy parks around the corner and we crouch low as we sneak across the lawn to the stage. He takes a seat in the front row while I practice.

"You are headed for a place called Oz," I say in a politician's voice.

"When Dorothy began, her intention was to find a way home again. Is that how you feel now? Do you really want to leave the security and comfort of Grosse Pointe South?" I ask a sea of nearly empty folding chairs.

Billy stands up and begins to clap.

"Wait," I say. "I'm not finished."

★ ★ ★ ★ ★

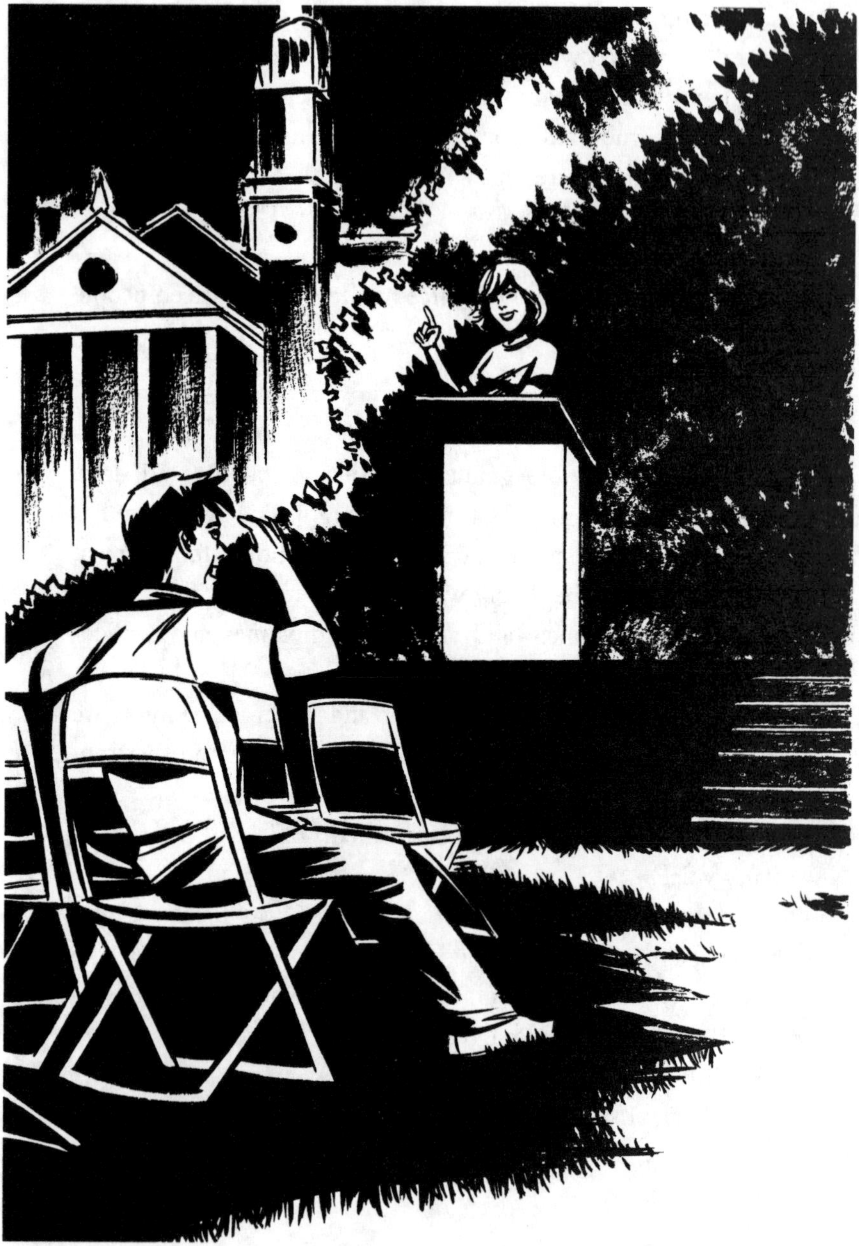

"I think this is yours." Katrina Krause is standing in front of me, offering a slab of cardboard covered in blue silk, the gold tassel dangling from the top. Despite the principal's warning, our caps flew into the air simultaneously as soon as the last name was read. It looked like a flock of birds heading south for the winter, then changing their minds as they fell to the ground. We'd been spending the last twenty minutes wandering around the front lawn trying to return hats to their rightful owners.

"Thanks," I say.

"I liked your speech," she tells me, fixing the bobby pins in her hair.

"Oh, it was stupid."

"No it wasn't. I could never get up there and speak in public like that."

"Really?" I say, pulling on my lip. "I don't even know what I was saying. I was just telling people what they wanted to hear."

"What's that exactly?"

"I don't know. That everything is going to be okay, I guess?"

She nods. "Well. I better go look for my own hat. They're threatening to hold our real diplomas until we turn in our cap and gown."

"I heard that too," I say.

It's the longest conversation we've had in four years.

* * * * *

The all-night, school-sponsored party starts an hour later at the war memorial. My fellow graduates and I have changed into the coveted seniors-only T-shirts made by the class council, long sleeved and white with every student's name printed on the back—even Mike Cleveland's. Every room in the war memorial houses a different activity. There's a movie room showing back-to-back comedies. In the basement, groups make sing-along tapes to their favorite songs. Upstairs, a fortune-teller holds our palms and predicts our futures. Later, we'll all gather in the auditorium for the hypnotist's show. To sustain us, there are tables of food scattered throughout the building, piled high with trays of cold cuts and bowls of pasta salads, iced brownies and toffee-walnut cookies.

I am refilling my punch glass, surprised that no one's spiked it yet, when I feel a tap on my shoulder.

"There you are," Billy Crandall says. "I've been trying to find you for a hundred years. Come with me."

"Where are we going? I'm supposed to record 'You Got a Friend' with Lucy and Jennifer and Christina in ten minutes."

"That is so lame, I won't bother with additional comment. Just come. This isn't going to take long."

He leads me into the ballroom, the same one we used to go to for war memorial dances in middle school. There's a DJ set up in the corner, just like I remember. The room looks much larger and I realize it's because we're the only ones here.

Billy closes the glass doors behind us. He nods to the DJ.

Eric Clapton's "Wonderful Tonight" begins to fill the room.

He grabs me around my waist and I forget about all the skinny Catholic schoolgirls who've competed for Billy's heart over the years. For this one moment, it's just me and Billy Crandall, turning slowly on an empty hardwood floor, not dancing really but more like a gentle rocking, as if we are at sea.

"This is how the prom should have been," he whispers in my ear.

I hold on, and I let go.

★ ★ ★ ★ ★

"So this is what Grosse Pointe looks like at dawn."

Billy and I are sitting on the stone wall that borders the back lawn of the war memorial, just a few feet from the waters of Lake St. Clair. Behind us, chaperones and teachers are setting up for the convocation that marks the official end of the all-night festivities.

"I don't think I've ever been up this early," I tell him, tearing a cheese Danish down the middle and passing him a half. We've collected items from the breakfast buffet to make our own picnic. The juice tastes especially tart, the coffee tough, the way I like it. I go in for a chunk of powdered doughnut, licking the sweet sugar off my fingertips.

It's the best meal I've ever had.

"Actually, I think you mean you've never stayed up this late," he says, smirking.

"Right." I stir a packet of nondairy creamer into my paper cup. We chew our doughnuts. "Billy?"

"What-y?" he says like he always does.

"You'll come visit me at school, right?"

"Emma, you're not leaving for three months." Billy's chosen to stay close to home and pick up a few classes at the local community college.

"I know. But you'll come, right?"

He takes a sip of his coffee. "Of course. It's only an hour and a half away."

The lake is calm this morning—slight ruffles on the surface like someone is snoozing nearby. Even at this hour, the humidity begins to brew, coating our skin. Billy clicks his Zippo open and shut, open and shut. He shakes out cigarettes from his pack for both of us. We light up for one last time as high school students.

Behind us, the adults hover over a faulty audio system. "Testing," they blow into the mike, tapping the head. It echoes across the lawn like a heartbeat.

It's a race against time to make our final event perfect.

"The fish flies will be here soon," I say.

"Yep. Every June."

"Some things never change."

Billy looks at me. "Some things never will."

13

Reunion

7:15 P.M.

"It's going to be just like a high school dance," I tell Lucy in the car on the way to the Grosse Pointe Yacht Club.

"Do you want to stop for a drink first?" she asks.

I make an illegal U-turn on Kerchavel Avenue.

★ ★ ★ ★ ★

7:49 P.M.

"What are you guys in town for?" our bartender asks. I recognize his face but can't remember his name. He graduated two years behind us.

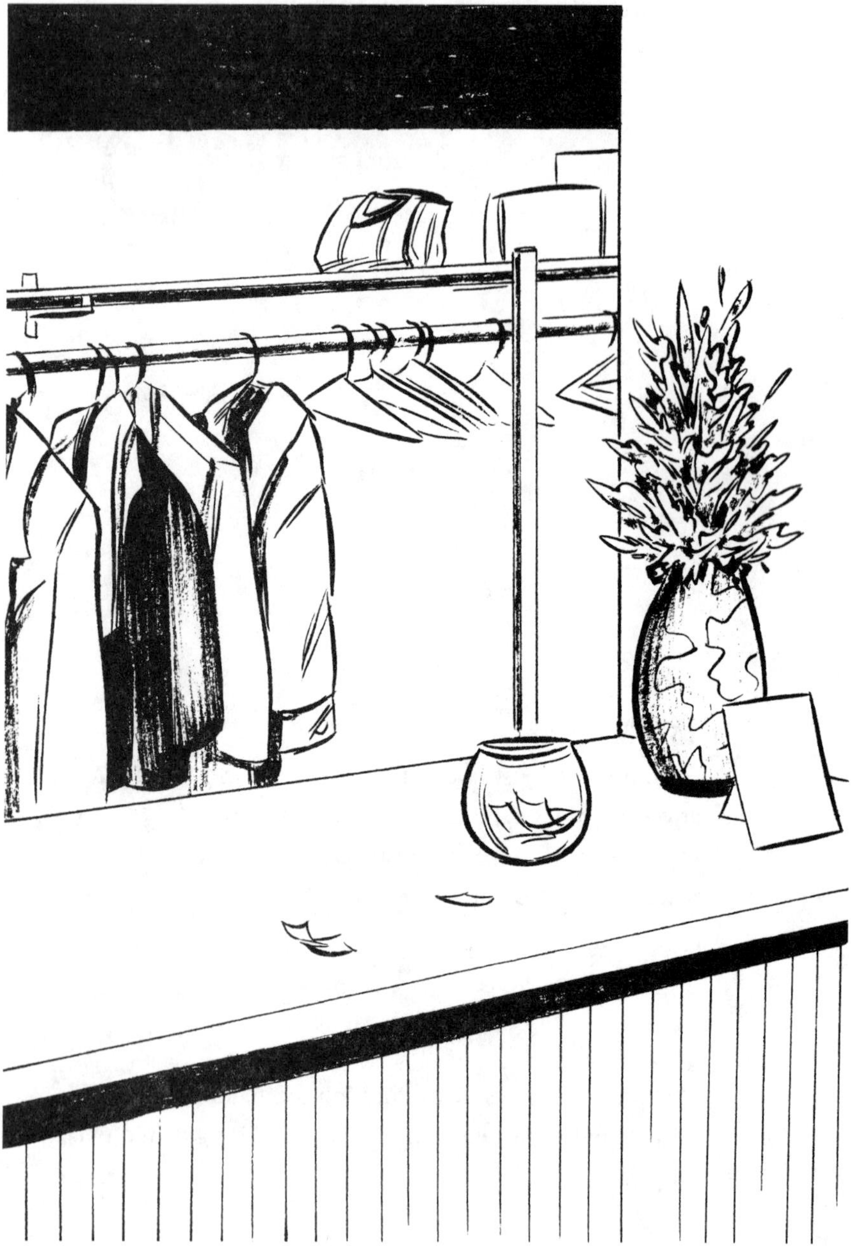

"Reunion," I tell him. "Ten year."

"Oh!" he says. "That's right! I saw it in the *Grosse Pointe News*."

We nod.

"Another round?" he asks.

We nod.

★ ★ ★ ★ ★

8:21 P.M.

We're sitting in the parking lot trying to decide whether or not we should wear our coats inside or just make a break for it. It's four degrees with the wind chill and we're parked twenty feet from the door.

"See," I say. "Told you it'd be just like a high school dance."

"I bet there's a coat check," Lucy offers.

"How very grown up," I say. "You're probably right." I flip down the visor and reapply my lip gloss. "Do you think they'll have name tags?"

"Of course," she says.

"I'm not wearing mine."

"You have to!" Lucy says.

"No I don't. It's not like I'm going to get a detention. Fuck it." The rule tonight, I've decided, is there are no rules.

"Ready?" she asks.

I have five $20 bills for the open bar. I have gum and plum-colored lipstick and a camera with a full roll of film. I am wearing all black because it's supposed to be "slimming."

I will tell people it's because I am in mourning over the loss of my childhood.

* * * * *

8:32 P.M.

The first person I see in the main dining hall is a very pregnant Christina standing next to a very pregnant Jennifer. They are both six months along. Their due dates are two weeks apart. They are both having boys. I wonder how they became so coordinated, if there's some bylaw that keeps them within five feet of each other all night.

Later I will tell Lucy, "They're supermodel pregnant," and she will roll her eyes in agreement. There are no bloated ankles or excessive weight gains. They just sparkle. It's almost like it doesn't count.

My instinct is to put my hands on Christina's stomach and I do. It feels hard, not squishy like my own, stretched and taut, like a coconut, like I could knock on it and hear a hollow echo inside.

"I can't believe you're pregnant at our reunion," I say to her. "Couldn't you have gotten knocked up in high school like a normal person?"

* * * * *

8:39 P.M.

"Where's the bar?" I ask Lucy. She points to a doorway behind a cluster of people, thirty or forty faces. There are a lot of suit jackets and cocktails in hand. Some are introducing spouses or passing around photographs of their children. Everyone looks strange, like a deck of cards spilled onto the floor, familiar but in the wrong order. I am suddenly grateful for the name tags that were indeed laid out for us on a table next to the coat check, white cards bordered in our gold-and-blue school colors and slipped into protective plastic sleeves.

"I'm not ready yet. I need a prop," I tell her, pleading.

"Keep your head down," Lucy coaches. "Don't make eye contact. Stay focused. Plow through."

⋆ ⋆ ⋆ ⋆ ⋆

8:48 P.M.

The bathrooms are in the farthest corner of the room, tucked down a back hallway. I don't really have to go, I just need to hide, stop, breathe. There are only two stalls and the door is closed on one of them.

It's like Russian roulette and I am standing in front of the gun.

I start making a list in my head. "Hi, how are you" and "Good to see you" and "How long have you been here," questions to ask in case I don't know who it is and need a diversion to steal a glance at her name tag. Maybe I can use the bathroom mirror in some way to cheat.

The toilet flushes. When the stall opens, it's Katrina.

"Thank GOD that was you," I say, hugging her with my gloss wand still in hand.

She laughs. "That's so weird to walk out and see you standing there putting on lipstick. I still remember how you put on your makeup in seventh grade. You could do it faster than anyone. You told me you could do it in five minutes or less," she says, washing her hands.

"I did?" I say. I don't remember this, but the truth is, the time frame hasn't changed much, except for tonight of course when I took an hour to paint over every mark and line I could find.

"Yes, of course. So check it out," she says, holding her bare, ring-free hand out to me. In her last letter, she told me about her divorce. "What do you think?"

"I think I owe you a drink." I hook my arm through hers as my anchor.

★ ★ ★ ★ ★

8:59 P.M.

"Tim Osborne just told me he's still in love with me," Lucy confides.

"Still? When was he ever?"

"Exactly."

"Wow. You got the 'I've always loved you' confession," I say making air quotes with my hands.

"Do I get some sort of door prize?" Lucy asks.

"Yes," I say. "You get to be someone's regret."

★ ★ ★ ★ ★

9:14 P.M.

I've discovered the bathroom hallway that loops around to the bar, an alternate route and less crowded. I sneak down my secret path for another meeting with my new friend Dr. Chardonnay.

"Nice, Harris. Walk by me and pretend you don't see me."

It's Billy Crandall.

"I just talked to you two days ago," I say, kissing him the way adults do as two girls come around the corner. Leslie Peters and Martha Moran—I'm getting the hang of this stealth name-tag reading. Martha makes a break for the bathroom, but Leslie is stuck in the hallway with us.

"This is sharp," Billy says, touching the fuzzy black collar of her coat.

"What?" she snaps.

"It's sharp," Billy says again. "It's nice."

"What is?" Leslie says.

"He's telling you he likes your coat," I explain.

"Oh," she says, exhaling. "Thanks." In the pause, she looks at our tags, reading our names aloud slowly, as if they were written in a foreign language. "Billy . . . Crandall. Emma . . . Harris. So. What are you two up to?" she asks. I wait for a yawn to follow the statement but she manages to hold it in.

"I've been living in Gary, Indiana," Billy says. I turn and stare at him as he continues. "A lot of people say it's a crappy town, but I really think it's got some character." Gary, Indiana, is a lot of things: an industrial wasteland, home of the Jackson 5, a dirty pit stop on the way to Chicago, but it is definitely not the new, beloved home of Billy and never has been. I decide to let him run with it.

"Indiana?" Leslie says. "Really? What do you do there?"

"I run an auto-collision shop off the interstate."

"Married? Kids?" she asks.

"Yeah, yeah. Got two, a boy and a girl. Well, they're not really mine but they are now, you know what I mean?" He laughs and nudges her elbow.

"Really?" she says. "That's nice. You?" She turns to me.

"I . . . I live in New York." Brooklyn, actually, but it's all I say, partially because I'm trying not to laugh at Billy's tall tale, and partially because it's the statement I've been coming back to all night. It's limited and brief, but what I've discovered in the past two hours is that anywhere past the Michigan-Ohio state line is too far away to know the difference or care. "What about you?" I ask.

"Well," she begins. "I don't know if you remember or not, I left after our junior year and moved to Texas."

"Of course!" I say. No, I think.

"So I already did the 'living-out-of-state thing' a long time ago."

"Right," I say, wondering when it became a contest. "So you're back in Michigan now?" I ask.

"Yes. I'm going to dentistry school," she tells us. I congratulate her on this accomplishment as her friend exits the bathroom. After a few polite courtesy nods, we go our separate ways.

"What was that all about? Gary, Indiana? You could have warned me," I say to Billy.

"I decided I wouldn't tell the same person the same story tonight. Keep things interesting."

"Beautiful," I say. "What else you got going so far?"

"President of the International Squash Club."

I wish I had thought of it first.

* * * * *

9:50 P.M.

"Is that Paul Hanson?"

"Yeah, I think so," Lucy says. He's six, maybe seven feet from me.

"God, I haven't seen him in a hundred years. He was so funny in high school. I always wanted to talk to him more."

"Did you say hello?" she asks.

"No," I tell her.

"Why not?"

"I just don't know what to say."

★ ★ ★ ★ ★

10:22 P.M.

"You need to put me in one of your stories," Hello My Name is Nick O'Toole tells me.

"Which one?" I ask.

"I don't care. Any of them. I don't even have to be a main character. I can be the character who dies early."

This is the first boy I ever made out with, behind a church in sixth grade. Two weeks later I dumped him because he only talked about baseball.

"So what are you doing now?" I ask him.

"I'm the sportscaster for the Fox station in Toledo," he tells me.

"Perfect," I say.

★ ★ ★ ★ ★

10:36 P.M.

Pregnant Christina comes up to Billy and me as we loiter by the bar. "Well. I just witnessed the strangest thing," she says with a Diet Coke in her hand.

"What's that?" I ask, on my fifth wine. I figure I'll drink for Christina too.

"I was standing by the bathroom with Stephanie DeMarco, catching up—"

"How is our Stephanie DeMarco doing, by the way?" I ask.

"You mean Stephanie DeMarco-Van Eden."

"God, that's just wrong in so many ways. Anyway, go on."

Christina was always the best at relaying gossip. "So Mary Greer walks by."

"Who's Mary Greer?" Billy asks.

"She was sort of quiet," I tell him. "Short brown hair, freckles."

"Anyway, Stephanie's like, 'Hey, Mary, how's it going?' And she just sort of looks at her. So Stephanie thinks maybe Mary doesn't recognize her and she says, 'It's Stephanie. Stephanie DeMarco.' And Mary says, 'I know.' And then she says, 'Isn't it funny how all the popular kids want to talk to you now?' and walks away."

We're all quiet for a minute. I'm certain I must have misheard Christina over the blaring DJ who seems determined to make someone, anyone, dance.

"Obviously, Mary's been planning to say that to someone all night."

"Wait," Billy says. "Who's Mary Greer again?"

"Can't miss her," I tell him, throwing back the last swallow of wine. "She's the one with the giant chip on her shoulder," I say.

She's me, I think.

I set down my empty glass and head to the bar for drink number six.

* * * * *

10:54 P.M.

What's most strange is not talking about who's in the room but rather who isn't.

In an alcove near the kitchen doors, I finally find something that passes as a tribute. It's just a few candles surrounding cards inscribed with the names of those who didn't make it. I start counting. There are far more on the table than there should be after only a decade—five, six, seven, no, eight names. It's not even the number of names that's so unusual, it's the way most of them left. It started with Mike Cleveland, and over the years, I'd heard of the others.

We still called them "accidents."

It's a small lie, white with comfort to erase any sense of mortality.

Nobody said much about the name cards throughout the night, as if making the truth airborne with our memories and our mouths would put us all at risk.

* * * * *

11:29 P.M.

"Last call," the bartender announces.

The end of the night had sneaked up behind us like a trick-or-treater.

"It all went by so fast, I felt like I didn't really get a chance to talk to anyone," I tell Billy, my words still coming out with minimal slur.

"When are you flying out?"

"Tomorrow."

"Why so soon? You never visit when you visit!"

"You know what happens when I overstay my welcome. I suddenly sprout a monogrammed blouse, zits on my chin, and a delusional sense of self."

"Wow, that last part sounded very textbook."

"I was quoting my therapist."

He kisses my cheek. "That's my girl."